SEDUCTRESS

SEDUCTRESS
EROTIC TALES
OF IMMORTAL DESIRE

EDITED BY
D. L. KING

CLEiS
PRESS

Published in the United States by Cleis Press, Inc., 2246 Sixth Street, Berkeley, California 94710.

Printed in the United States.
Cover design: Scott Idleman/Blink
Cover photograph: Lise Gagne/Getty Images
Text design: Frank Wiedemann

First Edition.
10 9 8 7 6 5 4 3 2 1

Trade paper ISBN: 978-1-57344-819-2
E-book ISBN: 978-1-57344-833-8

Contents

INTRODUCTION

I admit it: I enjoy the vicarious thrill of the fantastical and the unexpected, especially when said thrills come with a large dollop of sexy thrown in. Of course that would make sense, given my obsession with sex and all things erotic.

But where, exactly, did the idea for a book of succubus erotica come from?

Regardless of how much I try to deny it, I'm a sucker for things that go bump in the night. I've been a vampire lover since my father introduced me to Bram Stoker's *Dracula* as a child, so the jump to succubi was a reasonable progression. Woman + sex + power = succubus and, let's face it, I'm always excited by women with sexual power.

I read a lot. I get ideas. A while back, I found myself reading a lot of succubus fiction—which naturally gave me ideas about a book of succubus erotica. Don't get me wrong, any story about succubi is, by rights, going to be sexy, but it won't be quite the same as erotica edited by yours truly.

So, what have we got? Sexy, immortal women with the

power to steal what they need from human beings through seduction. And what exactly is it they need from human beings? Life force; they need the life force that comes from sex. You see, a succubus needs sex to live. Yeah, that's right. I'm talking about *the Big O*.

I feel it only fair to warn you, I'm talking about thieves of life; things can get a bit dark. I'm not saying all the stories are dark. There's a good balance of light mixed in with the dark, a balance of sad with the sweet, harsh with loving. You'll find an imaginative, eclectic mix here. As in V. K. Foxe's "Street Hustle." Occupy Wall Street's got nothing on this succubus. And then there's "Star-Crossed." I think the Bard, unlike Evan Mora, actually meant for his unfortunate lovers' end to remain tragic, but then, you never know.

If you're looking for a woman who'll brook no nonsense, look no farther than N. J. Streitberger's "The Girl on the Egyptian Escalator." She wants what she wants when she wants it—and she'll get it, too.

Succubi are, of course, the ultimate in dominance. Whether they're scary, sweet, loving or rough, they're in control. Even if the *meal* thinks he or she's in control, in the end, it's all about the *Daughter of Lilith's* needs.

Whether you're into femdom or just really sexy women, these stories are sure to satisfy. I can promise an erotic charge and sexual heat with each one. After all, that's what you came for, right? So, prepare for a wild ride into the world of immortal sex. Remember: She's had eons to practice. She knows how to take you there—and keep you there—until *She's* had enough.

D. L. King
New York City

HARVEST

Aurelia T. Evans

D evon threw the rune stone into the small fire burning on the concrete floor.

His heart quickened, thrumming excitement through his unrepentant erection until it was hard, burning coal under his robes.

Perhaps he should have tried less dangerous spells first, but he didn't want to mess with boring fundamentals like calling the winds or casting a glamour. Ever since he found his stepfather's *Book of Shadows* in the trunk at the foot of his parents' bed (technically under lock and key, but Devon knew where the key was) and read about the Summoning of the Succubus, Devon knew he wanted to do it. It had been torture just to wait this long for a holiday from school when his parents would be out of town, and it had taken him weeks to find a place to cast the spell, then clear the warehouse of transients.

The *Book* had a drawing that took up the length of the page, a late-nineteenth-century wet dream of a winged she-demon. In a small gloss near her waist, the author of the spell wrote: *The*

*rune cast submits your request to the underworld—take care
with your choice.* The Futhark rune he had chosen, Jera, meant
"good year" or "harvest." Oh, god, he hoped so.

The fire burned purple then shot up in a column of light.
Devon squinted as a shadow split the column in two then began
to obliterate the light. The spell had worked; the succubus was
coming.

Jera thought that the days of being summoned by horny power-
hungry wizards had ended with the industrial revolution. Spirits,
demons, magic...these were mere fantasies from a superstitious
age. And that was how the spirits, demons and other magical
entities liked it. No more interruptions, no more barred gate-
ways. The world was a succulent garden of desperate, depressed
men to consume, and no one ever suspected that their dream
lover was real. She and her sisters and brothers could steal the
gasping breath of their victims' satisfaction with impunity and
move on without being hunted.

However, now she was dragged from one side of the world to
the other for the whims of whatever wizard called her.

She stepped from the light and braced herself for magic to
collar and claim her.

But there was no wizard kneeling on the floor—only a boy.
A young man who had barely filled out his shoulders and whose
dark brown eyes were guileless. He stared up at her with mouth
wet and pupils huge, and he did not quell her.

The tension that yoked her shoulders subsided. Jera was
called, but she was not snared—suddenly her evening seemed
much more promising.

Devon had attended a few frat parties the last two years. Tipsy
sorority girls were once the epitome of sexual aspiration, and the

times he'd had them made up his prime accounts of conquest.

He knew, though, that nothing would compare with what was before him now. Silver-studded straps at the tops of her legs framed her bare cunt; boots of thin leather, like a second skin, stopped mid-thigh and laced tightly over bare flesh down the sides, ending in sharp stiletto heels; a latex harness clung to her breasts just below her nipples and lifted them up to display every square inch of their firm, lush expanse.

As she stared down at him, she unfurled massive, leathery black wings tipped with curved claws like obsidian glass. A long, black tail waved sinuously behind her. Eyeliner-edged eyes glowed deep crimson, the color of fresh blood on white porcelain. Her wet painted lips were the same color. Black hair that glowed amber in the firelight draped over her shoulders and brushed the sides of her breasts and the upper curve of her ass.

And she was all his.

Entranced, he stood and reached out to feel one of those perfectly ripe breasts.

"Ow!" His hand jerked back. A welt reddened and swelled from where her tail snapped over it. "What the fuck?"

"Did I say you could touch me, boy?" the succubus asked. Her voice purred, making the little hairs on his neck stand deliciously on end.

His tongue felt thick as he furrowed his brow. "But I thought..."

"You thought what?" she said, teeth white and grin feral as she stepped with a sharp click toward him. "You thought you would summon Jera and she would fall to your feet?"

Unseen hooks jerked him off the ground until he hovered before her, his arms and legs spread. The empty room echoed with the sound of his robe ripping. It fell in shreds onto the floor.

"But...but you're not supposed to..." he stuttered.

The succubus laughed, a low and dark sound like a silenced gun. "You're just a child. A child playing fantasy games. Well, boy, I'm not a game."

"You can't...you can't hurt me," Devon said. Exhilaration iced into fear. "The *Book* says you can't do anything to me if I call you like I did."

Her hands slid up his fluttering abdomen, and Devon recognized animal hunger in her eyes as she inspected her hung meat. "The pentacle only keeps me from killing you. But you called for Jera. You may have believed that you would collect a bountiful harvest. What you did not understand is that you are the field. And *I* shall reap what you have sown."

"I called you, and I'm your master now. Let me go!" Devon cried desperately. He hated the sound of his voice, which seemed to have regressed back to the awkward adolescence he thought he'd left behind.

"Are you sure?" she asked, right before her scarlet lips closed over the head of his cock. He groaned, the rush of arousal faster on a wave of adrenaline. She slipped down the length of his cock for what seemed like eternity. Finally, her lips brushed pubic hair at the base. Her throat convulsed around the head every time she swallowed, and her saliva dripped down his balls.

Devon was so lost in the sensation that he did not notice the leather straps springing from Jera's hands like vines, insinuating themselves around the base of his cock and tightening at the top of his balls to pull them down.

"There," she said, cat-smiling at him before wiping her chin. "Now we have all the time I want."

"Fuck!" Devon screamed, frustration and terror battling each other for dominance. His cock was swollen above the leather, bound against ejaculation, bound into sustained sexual urgency...and he realized that she could leave him like this for days if she so chose.

He was completely at her mercy.

"Do you still want me to leave?" Jera asked. "I'm sure someone will find you in a day or so, and in such a state."

"No!" the boy shouted. "But..." His eyelids lowered. "Please," he whispered, "don't hurt me."

She gently lifted his chin so that he looked in her eyes.

"I *will* hurt you. But in the end..." That predatory smile again, like the glint of a sharpened blade. "It will be more pleasure than you have known or will know again, made more potent by the fact it cannot kill you."

Jera began to circle him, folding her wings back and surveying her prey. She stroked the broad, unblemished skin of his back. His shoulder blades twitched at her touch. She pressed a kiss to that perfect back; her dark red lips left no stain.

Her tail whistled through the air and marred the unmarked flesh. He jerked in his invisible bonds, yelling. Jera smiled—she had hoped he was a screamer. The welt striped over his right shoulder blade and was soon joined by a second, then a third. The skin split with the pressure, and the whiptail smeared each garnet trail of blood as it surfaced. He shouted after every stroke. As she completed her circle around him—striking him all the while—she curled her tongue to taste the tears in the air. But she also curled her hand over his saliva-slick erection.

He still cried out when she hit him, but after the fifteenth blow her hand tightened around him, and every time he flinched his back away from her, he also jerked his hips into her hand. His face flushed and glistened from tears, but his cock flushed and glistened as well. Both his eyes and his slit wept.

Jera circled around him again to view her handiwork. Saliva slipped from the corner of her mouth, and she licked it as she stared at the crisscross of rent flesh. Her cunt clenched as she came in closer to press her breasts against him. Her hands gripped his hips, and she rubbed herself lower. Her tongue slid out in a long, flexible, serpentine curl, and she laved the length of one line, shivering. He was young, healthy—a robust vintage. Jera had always been a merlot woman.

She shifted still lower.

His back was a mess of stinging warmth cooling where he bled. He hated that he was crying, hated that he screamed. But beyond the pain, his balls still swung with full weight and his cock still twitched desperately. Where she caressed him, the pleasure was amplified fifty times. Then the whip-snap of her tail—pain amplified fifty times.

She seamlessly brought his confused body back into pleasure, even through the stinging, as she pressed those marvelously soft breasts against him. He felt their weight as they dragged down his back, the hard nubs of her nipples catching on the raised welts. Then that tongue—as good as a blow job in a closet, and all she was doing was licking his back. Her saliva kindled the stinging anew. Tears leaked from the corners of his eyes as he threw his head back.

It felt like the world had narrowed to just this broad, echoing room and the woman whose tongue now slid between his buttocks to touch him in a place he had never been touched, never imagined wanting to be touched. If there had been anyone else there or if he had half a wit left, he would have protested. But it was much too good, and he shouted from the spiked lightning pleasure that coursed through him.

That tongue also curled around his drawn testicles, and that was when he realized how long it must be to rub against his asshole and squeeze around his balls. She tugged him sharply with a little giggle, and his mind's eye showed him what she must look like, her tongue now wrapping around the base of his cock. Then the tongue withdrew sharply back into Jera's mouth, and she came back around him.

"Please," he whispered. "I need..." His hips canted fruitlessly. He thought that if he did not come, he would explode, just burst at the seams like a dropped water balloon. But she simply shook her head and laughed. His eyes were drawn to the way her blood-smeared breasts jiggled. To the glimmer of moisture between her thighs.

With a twirl of her fingers, the bonds that held his ankles and wrists pulled him so that he was almost horizontal in the air. Hot precome dripped like bitter candle wax on skin stretched tight over blood-engorged flesh.

"My dear boy," she murmured. Her bloodstained tail caressed his cheek. Then the tip probed at his lips.

"Suck," she said, tugging at his cock. He yelped, and she forced her tail into his mouth. He could taste his own blood and the strange, smooth texture of the appendage itself. "Make it nice and wet. You'll have it in your ass soon."

Devon's eyes widened, and he could feel his ass clench tightly against the thought. But the more she plundered his mouth, the better the feel of her tail on his tongue. Soon he slavered over it, thrusting up to take that tail in as far as he could.

Jera threw back her head when he did. He moaned like a schoolgirl with her first vibrator, her tail gagging him and drawing the moans in heady hums to her cunt.

He attacked her tail with a fervor that made her mouth water as she imagined other places to which he could apply that

youthful vigor. She pulled her tail away and smiled when he
whined in protest. It swayed before her face as she inspected the
more than satisfactory work he had done. She could get used
to this; to this dear, ignorant and awake child instead of the
dream-drunk men she usually consumed.

"Good boy," she purred.

Her tail brushed his scrotum, then slithered until the tip
slipped into his hole. His eyes were round, the haze of lust
clouded with fear. Jera's tongue slid from her mouth to wrap
around his cock, sliding sinuously back and forth, round and
round his length until pleasure hit him again, and she pressed
in further.

She knew she'd found his prostate when he screamed, his back
arching and her tongue meeting with a fresh draft of moisture.
He thrashed from side to side against his restraints now that the
pleasure of her touch overwhelmed his virgin ass. Those beautiful clear eyes filled with confusion and unadulterated *need*. She
could not kill him like she did many of her other victims...but
she could give him the next best thing. She drew back from his
cock so that it jutted free, a rock-hard pillar. She wanted to see
all of him, debauched, debased, disillusioned, delighted.

"Remember who your master is, boy," she said, bringing her
right wing claw to his inner left thigh. "Remember who showed
you where you belong, where you *need* to be."

The echoes of his cries crisscrossed in the air like the welts
on his back when she dug that claw in and began tail-thrusting
in earnest. He was reduced to a rutting animal torn with one of
the most basic of needs.

Her tail continued to pound into him as she slowly lowered
him to the floor. With her carved artistry completed, she straddled him. Her juices dripped onto his stomach in hot pools. The
boy gazed up at her now with everything stripped away but that

which she gave him. The complete submission before her made her cunt contract tightly around nothing. He was ready for her, but more importantly, she was ready for him.

"You will like this," she hissed. She positioned herself over that swollen erection and sank down. Her tail paused inside him when he thrust up the rest of the way. This time it was she who cried out, the pleasure rippling through her. This was what she needed, what she craved.

Her wings spread to balance her as she began to ride him in earnest, thighs flexing and breasts bouncing with the force of it. After all her efforts, she was so very close. Her tail began to move in him again. His body was taut and defined and helpless beneath her, and she rode him at a galloping pace he could not match. Her cries became falcon screeches, and her glamour slipped for one moment. She knew what he saw—something perhaps not so lush, something rough, harsh, mean. She was the mantis, the widow, the vampire, the demon, and she was always so hungry, always seeking that which could satisfy that hunger...for a little while.

Her nails dug into his abdomen, and she released him from all of his restraints. When the bindings around his balls and cock snapped away, his mouth opened. Air expelled from him but no sound, just his entire body releasing its tension through the organ inside her. Pulse after pulse, hot and urgent, filled her where she devoured him. Jera's orgasm paralleled his. Her body writhed and pounded down on him, her tail still fucking him and stimulating his prostate, to draw every last ounce of his seed into her.

Men never understood how an orgasm could seem to last forever until she had them in her grasp. She could not have the boy's life spirit, so she would take what life she could.

Her cunt sucked at him, clenching that still spurting cock.

His eyes rolled back with a haze not of pleasure but of exhaustion. The life within his ejaculate, and what sexual energy he had left, filled her and made her hot with fever. When there was nothing left to suck out, she slowed, stilled and stretched, reveling in the flood of power within her.

She stood—no juices dripped down her thigh. She had swallowed every drop.

The boy had passed out. His soft cock rested against his bloody thigh, where two arrows interlocked. Her symbol: JERA. Maybe with her mark, the child would learn his lesson about magic.

Jera stroked his damp brow—she was almost glad she could not kill him, although she was already hungry again because of it. The spell that he had cast, however, dismissed her as firmly as it had summoned her, and she stepped back into the light.

Six undisturbed months later, she felt herself summoned once more. This time the magic was more powerful but still familiar.

When she stormed out of the light, she was ready to set upon him without restraint for being so thickheaded that he could not even learn a simple lesson. Magic that powerful was not meant for someone so dull.

But then she saw the naked form, the scarring on his thigh displayed to her gaze, and his cock and balls restrained not with magic but with a leather harness and cock ring. He had purchased it specifically for when he summoned her again.

He knelt, his expression open and wanting.

"Please," he said. "I need it again."

Jera's wicked mouth widened, and her teeth were sharp on her tongue as she stepped forward to claim her harvest.

A SURPRISING SUMMONS

Kaysee Renee Robichaud

When Konstantin's clumsy spell craft called her from the pit, the succubus did not expect to find herself confronted with the most unusual summons of her one hundred years. She clawed her way across the void and through the gauzy veils between her home plane and the mortal world.

The year was 1988. The city was a sprawling metropolis named for a long-forgotten duke. As she entered the world, Loreline found herself bombarded with wails. The mortals screamed about wars and increasing prices, scandals and poverty, starvation and all the same things they always bemoaned. She materialized inside a chalked circle, in a cramped studio apartment overlooking streets, trees and other anthill-like dwellings.

Konstantin was a lean man with curly hair and a trim patch under his lip. He wore loose, shiny pants and nothing else. His chest was toned, his belly almost nonexistent beneath a six-pack. He was thirty-six years old, a social smoker and lonely.

The last was a given. All mortals who called succubi were lonely.

Sifting through his surface thoughts, she found all she needed to assume the desired form. A nineteen-year-old girl with broad hips, blue-green eyes and round cheeks; bookish though intense. She added a few touches from his darker desires: black hair, an indeterminate Euro-trash accent and full lips. For a wardrobe, she fashioned spidery-framed glasses and an arterial-red gown, slit high along her thigh.

He smiled when he saw her. Smug, unfazed, unsurprised. *Bastard*, she thought. *I will enjoy taking your essence.*

"Welcome to my sanctum," he said.

"Thank you for having me," she said. The words were right there in his thoughts, and he approved of the accent, which turned *having* into *havink*. It all seemed rather prosaic, but the summoner's desires were key. "You vant to let me out of this, yes?"

He spoke the three charms, and Loreline pouted.

"Protections, now? Vere," she asked, "is your sense of adventure?"

"Safely subservient to my self-preservation."

She smiled. "I like men who understand subservience."

He blushed at this. Blushed! *Not so smug now, are you?* With a wave, the barrier around his summoning circle vanished, and she emerged. The three-inch steel heels on her conjured black-leather ankle boots clicked like switchblades opening.

"You're amazing," he said, and then shook his head at his own idiocy.

It was almost cute. She smiled at him, and said, "You don't need to woo me, mage. I'm here, your bed is there and your desires are plain." In fact, he was thinking about the way her gown would slide down her shoulders; about the revelations to come: the soft skin of her breasts, the goose pimples on her areolae and her firm nipples, the smooth flesh of her stomach and everything lower....

She raised her fingers to her shoulder and snapped, as though undoing a button. The fabric dropped with a flourish.

His eyes considered the crimson pool suddenly surrounding her boots. He knelt, then, rubbing the gown between his thumbs and fingers. "It feels so real," he said. Another surprise. Wasn't he inflamed with lust? No other man she had come to had paused for niceties.

His eyes roamed up from the conjured cloth to her boots, her calves, past her knees to her pale thighs. His gaze lingered on her dark pubic bush for a moment, before meandering higher, past her slightly round belly and full breasts, all the way to her imperious eyes.

She reached down and tousled his thick hair. It was a spontaneous gesture, not something plucked from his thoughts, and yet he responded to it with a soft, pleased sigh. Men throughout the ages had responded to such acts; even the worst of them— the most ambitious or the most corrupt—wanted something tangible to remind them of simpler times. A maternal demonstration.

After a moment, though, she caught his hair in a fist and turned his face to her groin. "Tongue out," she said, and spread her legs enough for him to catch her scent. "Taste me." She eased closer, until her sex moistened his nose and lips and then his tongue.

He dropped her dress and reached up, catching her ass with both hands. She made all the sounds he expected, enticing him further.

He assumed control then. Pulled her to the floor and fumbled his shiny pants open and down. Three kicks freed the right leg.

A squirm and shove freed the left. His cock was firm, slender but long with a curve to the left. He kissed her body, attentive to her shoulders, neck and lips, but shy about suckling her bosom. He was eager, though, to kiss her belly and lower. She eased her legs over his shoulders, when he slid low enough. He nibbled the insides of her thighs. He brushed the tip of his nose across her pubic hair and then spread her sex with one hand to best lick her clit. His fingers found their way inside and stroked, probed, delved, explored.

When Konstantin's mouth returned to her conjured sex, Loreline moved in time with him, exhaling and growling—but not for show, she realized with a start.

When she squeezed her thighs around this man's head, when she caressed her own material form, when the electric sensations evoked smiles and warmed her, these were real responses.

Succubi were beings of passion and energy who could adopt physical forms as desired. There was little about nerves or sensation to the forms. They responded instead to less tangible sensations. As talented as Konstantin's fingers or mouth might be, his real strength lay in his passion. It was strong, and brilliant as the sun.

He moved her legs farther apart, panting for more. Rising, he pulled her to her feet. He led her to the bed, and there he eased atop her, whispering almost loving words before his cock spread her pussy's lips and entered. She clutched at him, her nails growing to points to better scratch him. He whimpered, but did not stop. In fact, this drove him faster still. She stoked the fires in his heart and head and loins, and bathed herself in radiant glory.

His dick trembled before his seed flowed into her, transformed and transferred into her ethereal phylactery as soon as it slipped from him, release contorting his face. Unlike the many times she had witnessed such expressions, she did not laugh.

She was too busy being swept away by the tsunami of his climax. It was unlike anything she had experienced before. Intensity close to pain. Her eyes squeezed shut to block out excess perceptions, but this did nothing to steal the intensity.

Across three delicious seconds, her body dispersed and resolidified half a dozen times. And when she returned, her face was wet.

Konstantin leaned back to kneel between her legs. "Are you," he asked, between gulped breaths, "all right?" The rolling sweat made his chest shine.

She shook her head *No*. When he asked what was wrong, she had no words to explain. How could she explain that a succubus was not supposed to be able to orgasm?

The typical summoners were burnt-out men, obsessed with their tiny fleshy bits and their own mortality. They were power seekers and explorers whose passions for sex played a subservient role to other desires. So little usable passion blazed in those men and women, Loreline had long ago decided orgasms were a myth. Even Crowley, the great pervert, had been too distracted to bring her to climax.

But Konstantin was not distracted. Konstantin was a world away from her expectations. His inherent *wrongness* somehow made the experience right.

"Why did you summon me?"

Now, it was his turn to lose words. His thoughts were a jumble. Loneliness and eagerness and wonder and pain. This same cocktail drove all sorcerers, great ones and dabblers alike. Konstantin was not special. Konstantin was just as human and frail and weak as every other man she had been with. Yet, he was also unlike them....

She put a hand upon her belly. By spilling his seed, he had

lost a little of himself. The protections had kept his essence safe, but no shield was perfect. She was almost sad to see him diminished, even this little bit.

He reached down to touch her, and his spell ended. The pit tugged on her astral cord, and Loreline vanished from the summoner's bed, returning from whence she came.

The pit was not the place of eternal torment mankind thought it to be. Oh, there were plenty of masochists flogging themselves and whatnot, but the pit was mostly a matter of distance. A place without gods or divinely imposed restraints—in the pit, all restraints came from those who dwelled there.

Loreline discovered her own torment. Orgasm filled her with joy, but the intensity faded. Memory remained, which was somehow worse. With great joy, she discovered, came disappointment and sorrow.

She could not quite replicate it on her own. The men who called her—far fewer in the twentieth century's waning days than in previous years—were power-hungry toads with cinders for hearts. They satisfied themselves and left her untouched.

Then, Konstantin summoned her again. The year was 1998, the mortals screamed about economics and presidential scandals and earthquakes and weapon testing and variations on everything mortals had always bemoaned. She flew to him with a mix of excitement and trepidation.

Soft, sensual tango music played on the stereo.

Konstantin was older now, hair streaked gray, sagging in places that had been tight before. The soul patch had vanished; his face was clean shaven. He wore dark slacks with tattered cuffs and dress socks that were threadbare on the toes and sole. He had scars, too. Slender white knife wound remnants on his chest.

In his thoughts, he held her as she had been. Nineteen and

dark haired and intense. She molded herself to his fantasy, but added a few subtle touches, advancing herself to twenty-nine. The cut of her lavender gown revealed and concealed in all the right ways. No shoes, this time. No need.

"Hello, again," he said.

"Hello," she said and nibbled her lip. "Won't you invite me out of this circle?"

"You sound different," he said.

She smiled, reintroducing some touches from the forgotten accent. "This is better, yes?"

"Yes," he said, "but before I invite you out..." He spoke the three protections. An interminable delay.

Here he stood, and here she waited, and his desires were obvious, and his heart pounded with excitement. The fires burning inside him were still strong, though not quite the blaze he had possessed a decade earlier.

"Come to me," he said, and she went.

She raised a hand to her gown to snap and release it. He caught her hand, brought it to his lips and kissed each fingertip. "Do you dance?" he asked.

"I do," she said.

"I've been learning Argentine tango," he said. "And I was hoping to..." He held out his hands for her.

Her appetite growled for satisfaction, but the spell compelled her to ease into his arms. Her right hand found his left. Her left hand found his shoulder, while his right hand slid across her lower back. She leaned in, finding the dance connection. The best dancers communicated without a word, through tension and slight shifts in stance or waist or arms. Ten years had not made Konstantin a professional, but he was practiced.

The way he changed rhythms or eased her into and out of *ochos* and stylistic flourishes, gave her a delicious sample of his fervor. Dancing stoked his fire, and this in turn carried her away.

Outside the window, the city lights burned bright enough to blot out the stars. Inside, the man's fires burned bright enough to blot out the city. For Loreline, they were two bodies moving in infinity, stepping and stopping, turning and winding and bending. The dance quickened her breath, started the conflagration in her essence.

Afterward, he undressed her and they went to the bed, and danced to different music. They loved slowly and built to a wonderful, fast fuck. She rolled him onto his back and mounted him. His hands squeezed her hips and she ground against him, as his passion rose higher and higher. She clawed at his chest, squeezed his nipples and smiled when he winced. She savored his pleading for more, for faster. His passion overwhelmed her before long, and she screamed her satisfaction to the ceiling.

He was not yet done.

They rolled onto their sides. She turned to nestle her ass against him, spooning. After a little fumbling, his cock found her cunt and the sex continued. She experienced a second orgasm, moments before he released. He draped an arm over her and kissed her neck, and she trembled in the afterglow. More intense than memory. He held her, though she longed for solitude, to best savor the sensations.

"I've missed you," he said, and she smiled.

She murmured something similar. And they lay together for almost five minutes more, before the spell ended and she returned to the pit. Joy lasted a little longer. Renewed memories served her well, until the inevitable despair returned.

Fewer summonings, as the mortal world eased from one millennium to the next. The mages who summoned her were unable to focus upon the fine fucking arts.

When the ten-year anniversary approached, she grew eager. Would Konstantin call her again? Would he still bring her to that delicious place? The day arrived and passed without Konstantin's summons.

Disappointment and resentment warred inside her. Memories were not enough.

Then, his voice called. She debated not answering, which was foolish. She wanted to use him again; she wanted to feel again.

It had been fourteen years, now. It was the last day of 2011, hours from 2012. The mortals whined about nations and poverty and the end-times predicted by ancient calendars and all the things they had bemoaned throughout history.

Konstantin wore his sixty years with dignity. Some men aged better than others. He retained that essential vitality. Now, his head was clean shaven and his moustache was silver. He wore a three-piece suit.

She constructed a body from his thoughts, taking slivers of the familiar—he'd had a handful of lovers since she had seen him last, and she took the better elements from each to mold her body, advancing it to forty years old. Her black gown was elegant. When he beheld her, his eyes shimmered.

"Hello again," he said.

"Hello, yourself. Invite me out of this circle?" Too late, she realized she had again forgotten the accent.

He did not seem to mind. "Of course," he said, "Come out."

"No protections?"

"I've decided to entertain my sense of adventure," he said. "How is it you get more beautiful, each time I see you?"

"I age well." They shared a laugh.

He led the way to a table, set for late supper for two. She ignored her own chair, choosing to sit on his lap, instead. They kissed, and she tasted his passion. It burned duller than before, but it was still quite present—a minor miracle—the rude world snuffed passions when it could.

Her hands caressed him through his clothes, slipping between the buttons on his shirt to find the skin beneath. His heart pounded in a weaker way; the trip hammer was less regular, now. Still, it pounded faster at her touch.

His hands urged her to rock back, and she did. In his pants, an erection stirred. "You're just the same, aren't you? No matter how this alters..." He ran an open hand from her forehead down her face. "You're eternal."

"Everything changes," she said, "but not so much as mortals believe."

"Mortals." The word brought a grim smile to his face. Then, he asked, "Is there more? You come from another place, but is there more for me?"

"I cannot say," she said, "for the ways and fates of mortals are unknown to me." Her lips found his while her hand trailed down to his crotch, to knead him fully erect. "Isn't this enough?"

His kisses turned hungry. They shed clothes and their sex was tender, yet still overwhelming. She rode him in the chair, and then they fucked on the floor, and then they moved back to the bed. When he took her from behind, she orgasmed the one and only time that night, but it was beautiful. His erection softened before he could finish. She kissed him back solid and then sucked and stroked him to climax.

She had the option to drain him completely, then. Without protections, there was nothing to keep his essence safe.

"You want to die," she said, "don't you?"

"I'm already dying," he said. "I can't think of a more preferable way to go."

"I..." she said and then changed her mind. "I'll miss the way you make me feel." Then, she closed her eyes and took everything he had, while the city cheered the arrival of a new year.

When Loreline left, Konstantin remained smiling up at the ceiling. She envied him.

SUCCUBUS, INC.

Elizabeth Brooks

Lucy paces slowly through the call center on her way to the client meeting, listening to the phone workers' conversations. Lucy likes to know that even the first tier of service is exemplary, that the customers are satisfied—and that the workers are, too.

Here's Miriam, the call floor manager: "Are you touching yourself, Robert? Already? But we've barely begun, and I have so many plans for us today... Of course I will, darling, but you'll have to take your hand out of your pants, first. That's very naughty, to start without me." Lucy has offered twice to promote her, but Miriam declined both times. There are certain advantages to her current position. She gets to break in the new recruits, a task she relishes.

At the next station is Heather, one of the newer recruits. She glances nervously at Lucy as she passes, and Lucy slows a little more. Heather is still not entirely assimilated; she was recently disciplined for letting her clients rush the calls. Lucy makes a note to herself to check Heather's call logs later and see if her call timcs have improved. She might need another of Miriam's "motivational speeches."

And here is Bella, only three months out of training and already outdoing some of the phone workers who have been with Succubus Incorporated for years. Miriam has already taken the girl aside for extra training, and has asked Lucy to put her on the fast track for a promotion.

They're not all girls, of course. Niko sprawls in his chair, openly fondling himself as his deep voice purrs into the headset's mic: "You like that, don't you? Yes, of course you do. I can tell by the way you move, trying to draw me even deeper inside. You're so tight, so hot. I want to take all of you, right now—but I won't, not yet. I want you to enjoy this moment." Niko looks up as Lucy passes and winks at her. She doesn't mind his lack of reverence; Niko has no ambition, but he is a solid worker and balances Miriam's sometimes excessive enthusiasm with the new recruits.

A set of heavy yet elegant doors lets Lucy out of the call center and into the Individual Counseling suite. The faintest odor of sex and sweat hangs in the air, and Lucy makes another internal note to speak to the environmental staff: it is important that clients are shielded from one another, even subconsciously. Each visitor must feel as if he is charting virgin territory.

A staff elevator, discreetly placed behind a bank of potted shrubs, carries Lucy up to the penthouse level. A wide lobby leads to a single ornate door. It isn't Lucy's true workspace, but a suitably impressive office decorated with tasteful suede and mahogany furniture and expensive knickknacks of crystal and precious metals.

The client is waiting, nestled deeply into the soft couch. Despite the half-empty whiskey glass in his hand, he looks pale and nervous, and his temples betray a thin sheen of sweat, like an addict not *quite* overdue for his next fix.

Lucy settles gracefully into the leather wingback chair across from him and folds her hands, steepling her index fingers. She waits, calmly, watching him, as he watches her in return.

Lucy has done this many times before. She follows each minuscule flick of his watery blue eyes, cataloguing her own appearance even as he does: the expensively tailored suit, black and gray with just a hint of red; the dark hair, elaborately and immaculately arranged on top of her head and held with only a slender pair of jeweled pins; the severe-yet-playful glasses that enhance, more than hide, her clear black eyes; the long, graceful curve of her legs; the designer shoes with their stiletto heels; the alabaster glow of her skin that makes her throat seem curiously vulnerable.

In all, Lucy creates an intimidating figure. She waits patiently until the client is fully aware of this and has begun to wilt even more in the heat of her gaze. Finally, she lifts one hand, without looking. A thick manila folder appears in it, placed there by her assistant, Jasmine. The client all but jumps in surprise, having entirely forgotten the blonde bombshell who guided him here earlier. Lucy smiles thinly, glancing at the folder only for show. She has already memorized the particulars of this client's account. "Mr. Field, I understand that you have missed several payments."

Field tries to bluster, which secretly delights Lucy. She likes it when they're spirited. "There's been a mistake!" he insists. "I lost my job, and when I called to explain, they told me it would be taken care of, that I could put the account on hold and that I wouldn't have to pay anything for a year!"

Lucy nods smoothly. "That is correct, Mr. Field; we understand that sometimes these things happen. We're willing to work with you to give you the breathing space you need to get back on your feet."

"But the bill came due anyway, right on the usual schedule!" Field is squaring his shoulders and sticking out his elbows, puffing up in a display of belligerence. "So I called back, and they told me not to worry about it, that I should just pay that one, and then it would be taken care of. But it wasn't! Every time, I called, and paid, and every time they told me it wouldn't be a problem, but the damn bills just keep coming!" Field is raving now, his face beet red with self-entitled fury. "There is no more money, do you understand? None! The accounts are empty, I maxxed out the loan against my retirement, I re-mortgaged the house! There's nothing left to give you soul-sucking vipers!" He begins flailing, trying to free himself from the couch's deep cushions.

Jasmine lifts the phone to call security, but Lucy raises a hand to stop her. "Mr. Field, please, there's no need to resort to name-calling. I assure you, I take our customer service policy very seriously. A hold *was* placed on your account, no fewer than seven times...but at the conclusion of each of those calls, you availed yourself of our phone-service. Is that not correct?" Field is silent, staring at her. He does not contradict her. "As I am sure you know, resumption of service terminates the hold, Mr. Field. And since you have missed your last three payments entirely, I fear we cannot offer you that option again."

"But...what do you expect me to do? I just told you, there's nothing left!" Field's anger has drained in the face of his sudden hopelessness.

Lucy lets the moment stretch, wanting Field to absorb every nuance of his damnation. She flips slowly through his file without actually reading it, watching him sidelong as the quiet rustle of the turning pages urges him to despair. Finally, when she can see he is verging on true desperation, she says, "Because you have been such an exemplary client in the past, Mr. Field, we are prepared to offer certain...nonmonetary payment options."

Field looks up, wary. "What kind of options?"

Lucy smiles. "Employment, of a sort. Jasmine, please take Mr. Field to the Executive Suite while I put the release package together for him to sign."

"Of course, Ms. Morgenstern."

"What kind of release package?" Field is struggling to stand again.

Lucy comes smoothly to her feet. In her heels, she is taller than him by an inch or so, and Field shrinks into himself a little, unconsciously, as he looks up at her. "It's all very standard," she assures him. "Succubus has a highly successful video line of 'real-life' encounters. Go on with Jasmine, and when I join you shortly, we can go over it in as much detail as you like."

The Executive Suite is, of course, designed to relax inhibitions and ensure that the client will not give much thought to the contract when it appears. The lighting is soft and relaxing. The air is warm and smells sweetly of cinnamon. The decor is silky and soft—except in those areas where it is steel and leather. The artwork is tastefully erotic. There is a generous wet bar.

Lucy prepares the contract and herself, and then waits. Field must have plenty of time to convince himself that having sex on camera is the easiest road to getting his debt canceled, to reassure himself that no one he knows will ever recognize his face in a Succubus, Inc. video.

When she enters the room, her appearance has changed. The prim spectacles are gone, though her ebon hair is still swept up. The power suit has been replaced with a leather push-up corset and net stockings. Her calves are now caressed by soft, buttery, leather boots with wickedly spiked heels. Field drops his highball glass when he sees her, but Lucy catches it deftly and drinks the remaining whiskey in a single smooth swallow, letting him watch as she licks a stray drop from her lip.

Lucy gives him an excellent view of her cleavage as she bends to place the contract file in front of him. His gaze is still on her breasts as she takes his hand and leads him to the loveseat, snuggling in beside him. His pupils are dilated, and his face is beginning to flush. "Let's go over this paperwork, shall we?" she purrs, her voice slightly husky from the whiskey.

"Um. Yeah," Field agrees.

Lucy's lips, painted with a red so dark it is nearly black, hover only an inch from Field's ear as she points out the various sections in a throaty whisper: debt cancellation, usage rights, local and international sales, penalties... He barely glances at the dense legal text before he initials and signs wherever she tells him.

Lucy turns one final sheet. "And sign here, and date... Thank you, Mr. Field." Lucy takes the pen from Field's unresisting fingers and schools her expression to hide her sense of triumph as she adds her own signature to the page. "Now then, let's get started." She takes his hand and draws him toward the bedroom.

He follows, but now that he has signed, his feet drag. "I don't recall a no-harm clause," he hedges.

Lucy laughs. "Well, you have been a very naughty boy," she says. "Don't you think you deserve a little punishment?"

"I...I guess so."

"That's one," Lucy warns. "You will address me as Ms. Morgenstern, or Mistress. Do you understand?"

Field's expression is uncertain, but his eyes are dilated and Lucy can see the bulge of his cock pressing against his pants. "Yes, Ma'am."

"Mistress. Not Ma'am. That's two."

"Mistress!" Field corrects himself quickly.

Lucy smiles and positions him at the foot of the enormous bed. "Better. But for speaking without permission, that's three."

Field opens his mouth to protest, but realizes the trap and closes it again quickly.

"Clever boy," Lucy purrs. "Now take off your clothes."

Field does as she commands. She watches, enjoying the slow reveal of his flesh, the evidence of his arousal. His smell permeates the chamber, musky and needy and irresistibly human. When he has completed the task, Lucy orders him to his knees. She sits on the edge of the bed and drapes her legs over his shoulders, pulling him closer. "Make me come," she suggests, "and I'll reduce your punishment count by one." She is wet already, just from watching him undress.

Field sets to work eagerly. His hands close over her buttocks and he buries his face in her mound. His tongue separates her folds and begins exploring, tasting her, feeling her textures, seeking out her sensitivities. His energy, now that he has committed himself to this course, is like a breath of fresh air. Lucy fills her lungs deeply and lets out a sigh of pleasure. She appreciates a client who knows his way around a woman's body.

One hand slides up her body to fondle her breasts. He cups one round swell, fingers as hungry for her nipple as his mouth is for her clit. He circles and tickles, teasing. A sudden, sharp pinch of her nipple echoes his teeth grazing over her mound, just enough of a scrape to sting. Her breasts and clit throb with sensation, now doubly sensitive to the flicking of his fingers and tongue.

Field draws the swollen nub of her clit between his teeth, and Lucy gasps as he thrusts a finger into her hot canal. His sucking is almost too hard now, teetering on the edge of painful. A second finger stretches her, and a third. His tongue is no longer teasing but battering her clit, attacking it from every possible direction, pounding with need. Lucy's hips twist, seeking escape from the sudden swell of sensation. Field's arm tightens around her, pinning her in place as he ravishes her with his mouth and hands, an exquisite violence that she cannot escape. Lucy lets out a soft mewl, and her climax strikes with the impact of a tidal wave. Her juices flood Field's mouth and run down his face, but he keeps sucking, his tongue never ceasing its onslaught on her clit, his fingers pumping in her like a piston.

As the crashing waves of her orgasm begin to recede, Lucy puts one spiked heel on Field's shoulder and pushes him away. "You earned that one back," she admits, smiling. "But you gain two more for putting your hands on me. No, don't look so upset," she cajoles. "After all, each count is an orgasm you get to have for us. How bad could that be?" Lucy pulls Field up onto the bed beside her and closes her hand around his straining cock. "Let's see if we can lower your count some more..."

Richard Field lies on the bed, too drained even to pant. The restraints are gone, but it does not matter, for he is too exhausted to move. He has no idea how long he has been in this room, or how many times he has been brought to orgasm. He has no idea how many are left to redeem on his account; the penalties accrue quickly, for the most minor infractions and violations of rules no one will explain.

The raven-haired executive (*Mistress Morgenstern*, he reminds himself) is not the only one participating in the filming. Her assistant Jasmine, a gorgeous, voluptuous blonde, came in for a few rounds, earlier. And then they'd been joined by a dusky-skinned man named Niko. Richard had nearly balked at that, but Niko had navigated Richard's body as if it were his own. Richard had ended that session screaming with pleasure and begging for more. After Niko, it had been a slender redhead named... Mary? Maryanne? Something like that; Richard is getting too exhausted to keep track of the names. The redhead had tied him down and actually *talked* him into an orgasm, and left again without ever so much as laying a finger on him.

He is still dimly amazed that he is not in agonies of pain from the overuse of his poor dick. Once before, some years ago, he had managed four orgasms in a single night, but he had spent the whole next day feeling like he'd taken a baseball bat to the nuts. He's done far more than that this time, however—he lost count somewhere around twenty—and he still feels fine. Well, his prick is fine. But he's so very tired. He feels drained, literally, as if his strength is slowly seeping from his body like so much blood. He wonders when they will let him sleep.

Mistress Morgenstern comes into his field of vision. "Why, Mr. Field, you're not thinking of dropping out so soon, are you?"

Despite his exhaustion, Richard's cock stirs at the sight of her, and surges into full erection when he catches her scent, like cinnamon and sulfur and sweat. "No, Mistress," he rasps. "Of course not."

He ought to be alarmed, he thinks dimly. Something to do with the contract. Something about the recruitment process? But he is too drained to decipher the words in his head, and anyway he would rather watch Mistress Morgenstern climb onto the bed and straddle his body as if she intends to siphon every last drop of his manhood out through his dick...

Lucy stands in the darkness of the Executive Suite, watching.

Jasmine enters silently, stopping just behind Lucy and to her right. "He lasted a long time," Jasmine offers. She has been

Lucy's assistant since the company's founding, and understands when Lucy will tolerate unasked-for conversation.

"Yes," Lucy agrees. "He was very strong. Did we get enough?"

"Everyone got at least a taste," Jasmine assures her, "even Heather."

"Good." Lucy is silent for a moment, watching the thing on the bed that is no longer Richard Field. "She'll be powerful; I want Miriam and Niko both on the Orientation team."

"Of course."

"And make sure you get her to Recruit Orientation before she wakes up. They always scream when they see the change, and I can't take it right now." Richard had been strong; as a newly awakened succubus, she would scream loudly, for a long time.

"Of course, Mistress." Jasmine pauses in her reach for the phone, solicitous. "Is anything wrong?"

Lucy grants the blonde a grateful, if thin, smile. "I'll be fine," she promises. "Just a headache; I think I ate too much."

IN THE SERVICE
OF HELL

Michael M. Jones

My name is not Alice. My true name is lost to time, buried deep in some apocryphal text or etched on some half-crumbled scroll. I've been many people over the years. Tonight, for this assignment, I was Alice.

The Velvet Trap is Puxhill's "baby dyke" bar du jour. Its main clientele consists of questioning housewives, curious coeds and other women figuring out their identity. It also attracts those with the patience or hunger for that kind of action. My target had come here every Friday for a month now, going home alone every time. This visit would be different. My orders demanded as much.

I entered the bar invisibly, drifting through the early evening crowd unnoticed and unfelt, drinking in the ebb and flow of the emotions already saturating the air. It was a delicious blend of anticipation and nervousness, desperation and arousal. So many women torn between desire and fear, teetering on the edge. I could wreak havoc in a place like this, with just the crook of a finger and the bat of an eyelash. I could break down reservations with a lick of my lips and leave a trail of aching, wet pussies in my wake. If I flexed my power, I could spark orgies and start sex riots. Unfortunately, that wasn't in my mandate. Feasting was right out of the question, as was anything that suggested I'd ever been here.

I found Rachel right where I knew she'd be: propped on a seat at the bar, sipping on a frothy pink concoction that did little to bolster her nerves. She was a cute little thing: a mousy brown-haired woman projecting a "don't notice me" aura, all but trembling with trepidation, armored in jeans and a gray sweatshirt. She watched the rest of the room with wide, dark eyes, and I felt her heart race whenever an attractive woman passed by. *Maybe this time,* she was telling herself. But never that time. She let fear rule her, and it prevented her from blossoming. She'd chewed the gloss from her lips, biting her lower lip in an endearingly nervous gesture. Though I'm not supposed to sympathize with the target, I felt for her anyway. She needed help. Too bad she was going to get me.

I stepped into the hallway in the back of the bar to materialize and reshape my form. Rachel needed a delicate touch, not the usual bombshell fantasy I usually brought out to play. I'd seen what attracted her, and I drew my look from a blend of those women. It was time to create Alice. A blue-eyed blonde, she'd be wholesome, charming and vibrant. The girl next door, with just a hint of danger. Flirty and playful, but subtly relaxing. A few years older than Rachel. I gave myself softer curves, a dash of freckles, a light-blue dress that clung to my body without being obscene. I wrapped myself in confidence and made my way back to the bar.

As I'd hoped, Rachel's gaze fell on me; I slowed just a little, giving her plenty of time to appreciate the view. I took up a spot halfway down the bar, well within her range of vision, and ordered a beer from the bartender. I flirted with the pierced, purple-haired woman as she slung drinks, but it was out of habit, little more. Every move I made, every laugh, every hair flip, was ever-so-subtly aimed at Rachel. Capturing her eyes, keeping her attention, fueling her innocent fantasies. I could feel her arousal, coiled hot and tight within her, aching for release. The desire seeped from her pores, enhanced by my own special gifts. I'd tapped into her unique emotional frequency; we were connected on a level she didn't even realize. I sat and drank and flirted, gently turning away other offers and opportunities, letting Rachel slowly simmer. I knew she'd never come to me on her own, scared and hesitant as she was, and I knew she'd be distrustful of anyone who came up to her with no warning. She was overcoming a lifetime of conditioning, chipping away at a fundamentalist upbringing that had clearly done her no favors. Family and friends and religion had all taught her something that contrasted with her heart's desire. All part of why we wanted her.

When I stood and walked over to her, I felt her pulse hammer, her breath catch, her sex clench. Beautiful. I breathed in her scent, and knew her inside and out. "I saw you watching me," I said. I placed my hand on hers before she could pull away. "It's okay. I don't mind. My name's Alice." My smile was soft and guileless. "I know exactly how you feel right now."

Under my gentle yet firm touch, and my soothing words, Rachel relaxed, fear subsiding to be replaced by attraction. Within minutes, we'd taken our drinks to a booth where we could talk at length. The story I spun was a patchwork affair stitched from a dozen other lives, designed to make Alice as sympathetic yet attractive as possible. I was a junior executive from an advertising agency, here in town for a business conference. I was single, recovering from a previous relationship. "It ended well enough, but we were too different to stay together," I claimed. I'd been out since college, but I didn't make a big deal of it. Experienced yet available, vulnerable but strong. Rachel's eyes lit up as we spoke, her protective shell cracking and breaking away.

I held her hands as she told me her own story, not letting on that I was already intimately familiar with the details. A good girl all her life, raised by strict, religious parents, always pushed to do what they thought best. Starting to break free in college, always yearning for something...else. Staying with her high school boyfriend for years, with everyone expecting them to get married someday. Finding the strength to stand up for herself shortly before graduation, refusing to go home to the life planned out for her. Breaking up with her boyfriend-turned-fiancé, coming to Puxhill to reinvent herself. At an utter loss ever since. I read her feelings: she was on the verge of giving up, of letting the fear take over, of running home to familiarity and safety.

I stroked her hands warmly, letting some of my energy seep through the skin, an electric tickle designed to further fan the flames of arousal. She shivered under the touch, and I knew I had her. "It's okay," I soothed her. "Sometimes it takes us a while to figure out what we want in life. What we need." I met her eyes, gaze both offering and challenging. She gulped and then nodded. While the subject had never come up in so many words, we both knew what was to come.

I took her back to the hotel room I'd secured ahead of time. Her apartment would have been too safe a place, too comfortable. I wanted her off balance now, in my territory and in my power. It was a short walk, and I held her hand securely the whole time, fingers interlaced for comfort. I bumped into her

now and again, every bit of contact sending another spark
shooting straight to her sex. I felt her, hot and wet, desperate
to be satisfied; that in turn set me off, her need intensifying
my own preternatural sex drive. My nipples ached, my pussy
tensed; I couldn't wait to have her.

The elevator ride seemed to take forever. Rachel clung to my
side, and I leaned in to place a not-so-chaste kiss on her cheek.
My breath whispered against her skin. "Trust me, sweetheart."
She almost stumbled as the elevator came to a stop, releasing
us. I let her enter the room first, the door clicking shut with a
devilish finality behind us. Rachel didn't get far, pausing just a
few steps ahead of me. I caught up, slid both arms around her
waist and pulled her back against me. Her breath caught, and I
kissed the back of her neck, nudging aside the short brown hair
to seek out bare skin. "God," she murmured. "Why did it never
feel like that before—?"

"Because it wasn't what you wanted," I replied. Her skin was
soft, and she smelled of lavender. I flicked my tongue against
the spot I was kissing, catching her when her knees went weak.
This woman was so needy, so ready; my tactics were almost
like overkill. Light a match, she'd go off like a firecracker. I
teased the waistband of her sweatshirt up, tugging it up along
with the shirt she wore underneath, exposing smooth pale flesh.
She arched back against me, a low moan of pleasure slipping
free from parted lips. "If there's one thing that makes me sad,"
I whispered against her ear, "it's seeing a passionate woman
too scared to live properly." Now my hands were on her bra-
clad breasts, cupping them through the plain cotton. Mentally,
I tsked. Boring, and predictable. Sometimes it's hard to feel sexy
when you're comfortable. I kneaded her breasts, and Rachel
melted against me, lost in a sea of conflicting emotions. It felt
good, but she'd been raised to think otherwise.

I was starting to lose her, as questions slipped into her wandering mind. My motions fluid, I spun her around, tugging sweatshirt and shirt up over her head in a tangled mess, throwing them aside. Before she could react, I kissed her fiercely, capturing her lips, pouring some of my essence into her. I filled her with fire and intensity and need, letting it flow through her veins, through her chakras, through her core. She squeaked, startled, but kissed me back hungrily once my magic started burning away her doubts. Her hesitation a thing of the past, she threw herself into the kiss with surprising strength. Her lips parted, her tongue teasing mine as she responded like a drowning man seeks oxygen. I gave it all to her, holding her tight to me, fingers raking her back. I unclasped her bra, and it fell free, held in place only by our chests mashed together. She rid herself of it without breaking the kiss and proceeded to rub her breasts against me, feverishly. Her nipples were stiff and demanding, poking against me.

I briefly entertained the thought that I'd gone too far in priming her. No, this was what a lifetime of good behavior and mixed signals got you, like a long-dormant volcano stirred to life. Having unlocked Rachel's passion, I now drank it in, letting her spirit flow like smoke through me.

Somehow, we ended up naked on the bed, clothes strewn everywhere in our progress. She'd been an almost aggressive participant, yanking my dress off of me, flinging her own underwear aside almost contemptuously once she discovered the lacy, impractical black thong I'd worn underneath. Flushed with desire, chest heaving, she was beautiful: unexpectedly curvy, with smooth skin begging to be touched and caressed. I smelled the musk of her arousal, intoxicating and alluring; as I pushed her down on the bed, I buried my face between her legs. I spread her lips and delved deep with my tongue, tasting and teasing her while she squealed and bucked and begged for more. I lapped at her pussy, sucked at her clit, nuzzled and moaned, driving her even wilder. She grabbed a pillow, pressing it to her mouth to muffle the cries of ecstasy. She came in a rush, her screams penetrating the pillow, music to my ears. As her thighs clenched around my head, I pushed that orgasm as hard and far as it would go, fingers and tongue working together to push her to the edge repeatedly. She'd been building for a long time, far longer than I'd known her, and this was just the start.

When she was reduced to a quivering, shuddering, crying heap, I relented, sliding up to pull her into my arms, to hold and stroke and kiss her. I let her taste herself on my lips, sharing in the unexpected joy she found from such an intimate thing. Confidence swept through her as she reveled in newfound freedom, and I further massaged her ego with gentle words and playful touches. Don't get me wrong: I love guilt sex as much as any succubus. It has a lovely flavor and usually serves a purpose. But the purity of Rachel's emotions was like a drug, a rush rarely found in my line of work. How could I not enjoy it? As long as I got the mission done, that is.

It didn't take Rachel long to recover. Soon, her hands roamed my body with increasing confidence, caressing my breasts and curves with joy and fascination. Though inexperienced, she learned quickly under my subtle guidance. I arched and moaned as her fingers found my sensitive spots, whimpered when she bent in to taste my nipples, writhed as she grew bolder still. Though my own desires aren't often a priority on jobs like this, I wasn't about to complain when Rachel's wandering hands slipped between my legs. I spread them for her, letting her explore the slickness of my arousal, the heat of my pussy. She slipped one finger in me then another, finding me soaked and ready. As she stroked me, I wrapped an arm around her, drawing her in for a hungry kiss. I arched my hips, offering myself to her questing hand, encouraging her to drive those fingers in deeper, harder, faster. She did so, filling me, curling and fluttering them at my moaned demand, quickly getting the hang of things. I rocked against her, thrusting against the fingers, taking more and more until the orgasm ripped through me. Her mouth swallowed my cry, and she accepted it with a burst of pleased satisfaction. Revelation swept through her entire being as she accepted, at last, who she was and what she wanted. It was the turning point, her defining moment, and I shared it with her through our bond. And yet, I wasn't done.

I urged Rachel into position against me, twisting until I could reach between her legs while she sought out the pleasures of my pussy with her mouth. I rubbed her clit, once again flicking at it with my tongue, and she returned the favor, throwing herself into the task wholeheartedly. Fuck, she was a natural, and I mourned those years she'd wasted in ignorance and denial. If her soul fell to sin, she could join the ranks of my sisters in no time. And yet, I knew that wasn't her destiny. Just an idle wish on my part.

This time, when she came, I was ready for her. I gathered up my strength and my power. As she orgasmed, with her emotional floodgates thrown wide open, I reached deep into her soul. I took what I found there: thin strands of shining silver and purest gold, wrapped around her heart. I unwove them, gathered them up, stole them away on a wave of bliss, without her ever knowing. I dropped back into my own body, in time to savor my own orgasm, letting it pulse through me until I was spent.

I cuddled with Rachel until she was asleep, before slipping free. I tucked her in, kissed her forehead, and whispered soothing words she'd never hear but would always feel. She'd never doubt herself again.

My task done, I returned to my true form. My skin darkened to an infernal red, huge blackened wings unfurled from my shoulder blades, my eyes grew ancient and soulless, and a barbed tail uncoiled from behind me. I gave the sleeping Rachel one last fond look, before fading away. I took with me her sainthood, that ineffable quality that might have driven her to a life of chastity and God-service had she returned to home and church. It was better this way: she would live a long and happy life and not rise to threaten us. She would not be a weapon in the hands of our ancient enemy. She would be...normal.

My name is not Alice. I am a succubus, an agent of His Infernal Majesty, engaged in the eternal cold war between Heaven and Hell. Mission accomplished.

Until next time.

BEFORE A FALL

Kannan Feng

During the long days of autumn in Hell, the blood rivers grow sluggish and even Caras, Hell's great heart, beats more slowly. Autumn in Hell is a quiet time to anticipate the howling feasts of winter, and we devils sharpen our teeth and our appetites with small battles waged in polite company.

Last year, I attended a moon-viewing party over the River Nekane. A hundred skin lanterns floated in the water, throwing back ruddy, sullen shadows, and I found myself in a veiled corner with Atemi, a councillor from the Ministry of Wrath, and Sweet, the pontiff of gluttony.

"You think too much of yourself, Aquila," Atemi growled, his moustache bristling like a volley of spears. He was enormous, half again as tall as I, and monstrous in the way that only devils who almost never venture above can be.

"I suppose I must," I responded, "It is, after all, only what is promised on my calling card."

"Very pat," hissed Sweet, "and entirely what one would expect of Pride's favorite son."

I smiled in response, smoothing down the lapel of my dinner jacket. Their taunts pleased me, and I could hear the fine thread of jealousy laced through their words.

"Pride has not Wrath's numbers," Atemi growled, "Nor do they even match those of Avarice. In truth, little cousin, as the light goes dark above, fewer and fewer can *afford* you."

"I've no interest in numbers," I said loftily, "but give me a moment's opportunity, and I'll burn your ears with the tales of the heroes and saints that find my price altogether to their liking."

"*Price?*" Sweet hid her face behind her finger-bone fan. "You speak of *price* like a fledgling tempter showing off his skin."

I started to reply, but a delicately taloned hand tucked itself into the crook of my arm even as the cool evening air took on a hint of musk and apples.

"Of what fledgling tempter do we speak?" the Queen of Lust inquired. "Has one of my pages behaved badly?"

Lust has never been a ministry or a holding; instead it is a country. The newest Queen of Lust was small, barely coming up to my chin, with skin like brown desert sand and eyes as black as wet charcoal. Her dark hair was twisted into an intricate series of braids and skewered with an ivory hairpin. All of Hell knew that her predecessor had met his death with that same pin shoved into his throat and when I answered, it was with careful courtesy.

"No one in particular," I said cautiously. "I would never breathe a word against one of your pages, Majesty."

Atemi and Sweet murmured their assent, but the Queen of Lust's eyes remained fastened on me. There was a faint smile on her face, and it made my heart beat faster even as a primitive part of me prickled with fear. Lust is older by far than Pride, and I knew that my masters would as soon sing choirs to Heaven as intervene against her on my behalf.

"Ah," she murmured. "You speak of the greatest of Hell's armies. Why, I'll tell you here that it is the kingdom of Lust."

"That speaks of pride to me, great lady," I said, suddenly reckless. "Don't dismiss us so carelessly."

Instead of showing dismay, her smile only grew wider.

"How splendid," she said, her voice dropping to a whisper that was meant only for my ears. "Are you willing to prove your claims for me?"

"Prove, Majesty?"

She beckoned me closer and I bent down so that her mouth was a breath from my ear.

"Let me see your strength," she whispered. "Show me how well-matched pride and lust can be."

She dropped a kiss on my cheek before turning away in a swirl of red silk. It was a challenge, but it was also a command.

My fingers drifted up to my mouth, and for a moment, I could almost trace the imprint of her kiss, sweet, hot and damning.

She came to my bedroom the following night. I waited for hours, from sunset until the stroke of midnight, and then she was at my window, clad in sheer silk and smiling at me sweetly through the barred glass. I could have kept it locked against her; it is the succubi's covenant that they will never enter a place that has not been opened for them.

It was stupidity to anger something like her, I reasoned, lifting the latch. *Worth my head and my precious skin to bar a queen from my chamber.*

I gave her my hand, steadying her as she stepped off the sill, and she rewarded me with a small smile that I felt straight to my core. I swallowed hard, and she laughed, drawing me toward the bed.

"Perhaps your spine is not made of iron after all," she said softly, tracing my heart line with a sharp nail. "Perhaps you are only flesh."

"I am only flesh," I responded, stung, "but I will not break."

Her eyes drifted half closed and she slid her hand along my inner arm.

"Aquila Varris," she said softly. "Most favored of all Pride's sons, unbeaten in all his two hundred years, and oh so very handsome..."

She went up on her bare toes to brush her lips against mine. A wave of hot desire rolled through my body, and I shuddered.

With a soft, subtle laugh, she ran her hands down my body. Her touch on my clothed body was light, but it left fire in her wake. She pressed a gentle hand between my legs, purring sweetly at my erection, laughing when it made me groan.

My hands came up to grasp at her shoulders, and I would have drawn her close if she had not suddenly shoved me sprawling to the bed. Her strength was immense, and then she was on top of me, straddling my hips and rearing up like a snake about to strike.

She was clad in a young girl's shift, but it was made of a pearl silk so sheer that I could see every shadow of her body underneath it. My hands came up to slide along her full hips, bringing her down close to my body before coming up to cup her breasts through the fabric. Her body was full and ripe, nothing but softness and sweetness until she made a sound that was too close to a growl and slammed my hands down to the mattress.

In the flickering light of the candles by the bed, I could see a feline satisfaction in her smile that showed she liked to hunt just as much as eat. It was on the tip of my tongue to ask for mercy, but I bit down on it, instead staying silent when her mouth brushed mine and the dark tips of her heavy breasts slid against my chest.

Her thigh slid between my legs, rubbing against my cock almost slyly. I bucked up against her before I could help it, but then I forced myself still again, my breath harsh in my ears even as she laughed. She released my hands and sat up, and if she were a mortal woman, or any other devil in Hell's great reach, I would have tumbled her underneath me and had done with it, but she was not, and I did not.

"Wrap your fingers around the bars behind you," she said, pointing at the headboard. "Do not remove them...until you have to."

I heard the challenge in her voice, tossed down lightly as a glove. Resolutely, I grasped the bars behind my head, feeling cool brass between my shaking fingers. It stretched me out and bared me to her hands and her teeth.

She looked down at me with her head slightly tilted, running a sharp fingertip along her full lower lip. As I watched, transfixed, she slid her finger into her mouth, suckling gently and in response, my cock moved, straining toward her.

It made her laugh and then she was unbuttoning my shirt, baring the skin underneath to her mouth and her clever fingers. She lapped at my collarbone like a cat even as she pinched my nipples hard enough to hurt. I stubbornly held my tongue and she raked sharp nails down my sides.

She eased her shift up over her hips and then, in a single motion, it was flipped over her head and cast away, spraying her dark hair over her shoulders and down her back. Her dark skin glowed in the candlelight and she stayed still for a long moment, allowing me to look at her heavy breasts and the soft round curve of her belly above the dense tangle of hair between her legs.

I could smell her more clearly as well. This close and naked, her musk was sharper but still there was the scent of apples.

Once they were forbidden, and we devils have never forgotten.

Subtly and slowly, she rocked on top of me, brushing her bare cunt against my clothed groin. I watched entranced as her pleasure made her blush, making the tips of her breasts harden and bringing color to her face.

I moaned and pushed up against her when she ground against me hard, and this startled a soft sound out of her as well.

"More," I heard myself say, and there was just as much plea there as demand.

Another sly smile and she squirmed down my body, her hands opening my trousers and pulling out my cock. She was rough, almost careless, and I hung on to the bars with all my strength to stop from reaching for her.

Her fingernails were bright pinpricks of pain on my hips as she held me still, and then her mouth was on my cock. It was hot, almost past bearing, and my body bucked up toward her. She growled deep in her throat and I could feel the punishing rake of her teeth. I caught my groan between my teeth, and my whole body shook with the effort of not pushing up for more.

Instead she drew back, looking down at me with a gaze that was almost tender. She moved forward again, kneeling over me so that her wet velvet center almost, *almost* brushed my straining cock.

"What is pride to you?" she asked quietly, running her hand up the center of my chest. I forced myself to concentrate on her words, even as her nails flicked my right nipple hard enough to sting.

"Everything," I responded, my voice husky in my own ears. "It keeps me standing when I would fall."

"Falling, though…would that be so terrible then?"

She lowered herself down to me again. I felt the prickly wet heat of her against the skin of my cock as she dropped her mouth to my chest to lick and kiss. I held as still as I could for her and, distantly, I wondered what kind of pride this was that kept me as still as a statue, as mute as a monk.

She lay down on top of me, her face inches from mine and her hands tangling in my hair.

"Oh, I do love you," she said, and when I looked into her deep eyes, I knew that she meant it. She might tear my heart out of my chest and eat it, but she would still mean it.

She leaned up and brushed her mouth against mine. The gentleness of the motion after her bites struck me like lightning. I parted my lips in surprise and her tongue tip pressed between them, almost ticklish.

She took her time kissing me, pulling my hair just enough to hurt, and exploring my mouth thoroughly with her tongue. I tried to remember her scornful words and the nicks and cuts she left on my chest and hips, but I could have drowned in her sweetness. It made me think of things that devils seldom get, and it reminded me that we always, always want them.

"What do you want?" she whispered, and I looked up into her eyes, almost too dazed to speak.

"I want you...on my mouth," I managed to say.

She wavered for a moment, but perhaps she had had her fill of denying me. She shifted upward and her hands were clasped lightly over my wrists. She knelt over my head, bringing her cunt close to my lips.

I tilted my head back, smelling her even as as I started lapping at her hungrily with my tongue. She was hot and wet, and the more I had, the more I wanted. She groaned and rocked against me and I only tongued her harder, long licks up her slit and quick darting flicks at her clit until her cries stretched into one long uninterrupted moan. With my mouth on her cunt, all I could think about was how much I wanted to be inside her, feeling those slick walls around me.

I didn't realize that I was groaning as well until she suddenly stood above me, stepping back so that she had a foot on either side of my chest. Her breath came hard and I could see the wetness on the insides of her legs.

"Have me," I found myself whispering. "Please."

I released the bars behind me, feeling the tingle of blood returning to numb fingers, and I wrapped my hands around the curves of her calves. The feeling of submission and shame was scalding, but it didn't matter. Nothing did, except for her.

"Beg," she said, her voice as hot and rough as the poison wind.

The words stuck in my throat, even as I sat up and buried my face in her thighs. Surely there was a limit, surely she could not ask for more, but then she grabbed a fistful of my hair and pulled my head back.

"Beg me," she repeated, but her voice was soft and longing. She wanted it as much as I did, I told myself, and perhaps that made it easier to bear.

"Please," I whispered uncertainly. "Please, please..."

"Please what?"

"Please love me, please *fuck* me, please, anything, anything at all..."

Once the words started, they would not stop, and I realized I was half wild and crying on top of it. I should have been dead of shame, but instead all I felt was a great raw heat in the place where my heart should have been, open to her and with a craving that was better, surely better than pride could ever be.

"Oh, darling, my beautiful, my sweet bright lover," she whispered in my ear. "I shall set you first in the stars of the sky..."

She pushed me back on my bed, straddling my hips. I felt her clever fingers wrap around my shaft, making me harder than I thought possible and then she sank down on top of me with a deep sigh of pleasure. For a moment I could do nothing at all and then my hands tightened on her hips. If she were a human woman, I would have bruised her, perhaps broken her bones. Instead she was the Queen of Lust and the sound that came from her mouth made me cringe with fear even as I bucked up into her.

I wasn't pleading anymore. Now I was only a rope stretched to the point of breaking, and my shouts echoed in the room like the howls of an insensible beast.

Time and space shrank down to what she was making me feel and even if I felt myself going slowly mad from the scent of her and the flesh of her, I wanted it to last forever.

She locked gazes with me, and I saw her dark, dark lips shape the word *yes* even as her body started to pulse around my cock.

I shouted as I came, spilling inside her as she dug her sharp nails into my chest. Even that pain was pleasure, driving me higher and higher until I was only ash, floating down into a silence so pure that I didn't want to mar it with my breath.

I could hear echoes in the air, moans of pleasure, and I wondered dimly if they were mine or hers.

She recovered before I did, and she sat up on the bed, gesturing me over. To my own surprise, I was capable of movement after all, and I crawled over the rumpled sheets to lay my head in her lap. I could feel her smile as she stroked my hair.

"Pride," I said finally.

Her hand paused.

"What do you speak of, Aquila?" she asked.

"What you're feeling right now? The power in your fingertips, the iron rod in your spine? That's pride. It's mine."

For a long moment, she was silent and I wondered if I heard my own death pawing at the door.

Then she laughed.

"What do I need pride for, hmm?" she asked, tracing my mouth with an idle finger. "If I wanted it, I have yours."

I felt a deep and yawning ache inside me as I realized the perfect rightness of her words, and before I could decide if I wanted to howl or laugh, she kissed me and I did neither.

STREET HUSTLE

V. K. Foxe

Bern knocked back his third beer as another girl swirled around on the main stage until the song's final chord signaled her retreat. By strip club standards, she was excellent, really, but this club didn't cater to the average. The cover charge of a hundred dollars kept out the various New York City scruff, though Bern had heard they'd considered knocking that down to fifty. Funny. If he'd been in charge, he would have raised it to two hundred. *Don't back down. Double down.* That's how he played it at work, and that's what had allowed him to put Hamiltons under the G-strings—when they worked at it right and looked like something he wanted to get close to.

The disembodied DJ told everyone to give it up once more for what's-er-name and to get ready because "Lucy's up next, and she's red-hot scorching!" A mindless ditty started underneath the tail end of his sentence as Bern tried to think of any Lucy he'd ever known who'd been red-hot scorching: no, no and...no. Did Lucy Lawless count? Then "Lucy" appeared, and Bern sat up, for she fulfilled the promise. She wore tightly laced red vinyl boots that came up to her fucking thighs, where her taut young flesh was quite insufferably perfect, the legs closing together at a shiny red thong. Up beyond her firm, flat stomach she'd captured her breasts in a blood-red gauzy something—nylon? Chestnut brown hair and darker eye makeup set off the carefully constructed devilishness that included long red fingernails, too, Bern noted. As the lights flamed along her lithe, strutting body, even her eyes reflected a quick red glint. She looked immaculate, like sexual heat personified, and in a body fresh, young, and begging for corruption. The faces she made as she drifted closer! She'd look intensely interested, as if she were the voyeur, the men on display for her, then suddenly she'd let her face fall into a soft rapture, freezing into a doll-like state that signaled to Bern that she must be available for play, and...poseable.

Bern fell into a gentle hypnosis, maintaining only enough sanity to make sure to slip her hundreds, so she'd recognize him as an easy mark: willing prey. In Lucy's thrall, though, they all were, swaying like cobras to her rhythm. Bern had been staring for a while before he noticed her long red devil tail, which hung limply between her legs but whipped out at them as she twirled around the pole; a nice touch, that. As she got on her hands and knees—no, elbows and thighs—to work her way toward another hungry voyeur, Bern wondered how it could possibly be affixed to her, as it disappeared too seamlessly behind the thong. He shuddered at the obvious conclusion, that she performed for him while penetrated. Too deliciously taboo, solidifying her as his top choice.

All the while she'd played with that gauze as she worked layer after layer off, stringing her arms together behind her, demonstrating how she'd prefer to be taken, no doubt. The girls, of course, were free to add bondage elements to their dance, encouraged even, but rarely did they manage to be so convincing. Soon the red gauze mostly concealed a hand, leaving her fingers free to slide down under the thong and *simulate?* playing with herself, and as she did, one jerk of her wrist pulled the last layer off, letting the heavier than expected breasts fall finally free.

She made him wait, though. She'd read his interest, but red-hot Lucy in those shiny boots stepped right on over to another guy, one who'd only plied her with twenties. She went to him immediately, not even glancing toward Bern. At least, not until the lap dance began. Bern had settled for Devaun, a leggy blonde creature enhanced by five-inch heels (who'd been a consideration prior to Lucy's appearance). As Bern looked over jealously toward the man who'd ridiculously managed to catch Lucy, he discovered her staring right back at him as she ground her hips threateningly over her chosen victim. She held the suggestive tip of her tail in her left hand. As Devaun tried to sway and satisfy him, Lucy forced his eyes and mind to stay with her, cruelly and purposefully depriving him of his full enjoyment of the blonde, teasing him with a promise of more.

Oh, he understood this clever foreplay now. Lucy had decided to milk them both for cash; she'd use the lesser up for whatever he was worth, forcing Bern to stick around and continue dropping loose change until she was ready for him. He could have played hardball and walked out to show her that nobody made him wait, but hey, he respected the hustle. That's the rule of the winners: make 'em pay as much as they can for as long as they will, then rip the rest away.

When the blonde was finished playing all around him, Bern gave her a cool hundred, adding, "And get me beer with it."

Patiently, Bern awaited their inevitable collision. His mind wandered to work, and he wrote a couple of notes to himself on a napkin. Sure enough, his once-stiff competition made a quick wallet check, then nonchalantly headed out. Aw, poor chap probably had to get his sleep for work tomorrow. Bern preferred to stay up all night and either run on adrenaline tomorrow or lock his office door and nap in his favorite comfy chair when things got slow. After another onstage performance sucking them all off, or at least their wallets, Lucy disappeared into the back and, a few minutes later, reappeared. She locked eyes on him from across the room, as the show lights for another girl were swirling patterns across the stage. A strobe flash caught her in mid-stride, the light springing off her glossy red boots, those red claws, and her eyes, red-tinted for one more flicker. Her determined stride in his direction, like a hungry predator, made Bern go rigid head to toe. He breathed out slowly, keeping his cool, and accepted her greeting. "Interested in a dance?" she offered.

"That's one thing I'm interested in." She still had the tail in, which thrilled him. She rocked herself over him, fluid as his assets, flexible as the yo-yoing stock market, and oh so smooth, sweet, and enticing.

She smiled, then twirled around and, somehow flicking the tail up into her hand, ground across his hardness. "What interests you, Stranger?"

"Other than money," he said without subtlety, "I collect pretty things."

"Money can't buy you love," she teased.

"But love ain't that pretty," he said, scoring a sigh of laughter. "What money can buy you, though, is time."

She twisted to place her head on his shoulder and whisper with hot breath into his ear, "Some people's time is worth more than others'."

"Absolutely," he agreed. "Anyone you'd *spend* time on, you should be willing to spend *money* on, too. Like you."

"Me?" she asked, swiveling back onto her feet to stand before him and freezing, once more, into that doll-like state of nonbeing, posed perfect with distant eyes and glossy, wet ready lips. The gauze around her breasts detached once again, the first strand swinging down, teasingly, across his slacks. Then she snapped back, fixed him with a stare. "My time will cost you." A challenge. "Either you're willing to spend five figures, or you spend time with five fingers." She made a quick jerking motion in front of herself, simulating a mocking throw of ecstasy that Bern felt viscerally as his own.

"Ten K?"

"Fifteen, actually." She winked.

"When do you get off?" he countered.

"That depends on you. My shift is already over."

Very sneaky. He made a show of paying for the lap dance and followed her out, though not through the main door. "This way," she whispered. A deal with a particular bouncer, it seemed, for she touched him lightly as she passed by, a single finger along his cheek that became a gentle scratch under his chin, turning his head to her. "Good night, Brut," she trilled, lifting an overcoat from a rack at the door and throwing it on. Brutus, eyes fixed on Lucy, didn't seem to notice Bern pass.

Bern raised his hand for a cab, but she slapped the hand back down. She pointed across the way, to an expensive hotel two blocks away. Even with the overcoat draped over her, Lucy had sway and those boots. Heads turned, yet she didn't notice anyone but Bern, placing a hand on his back, rubbing him gently and allowing her hand to slide lower, lower. "You should tell me what you like," she said softly as her hand slid behind the waistband of his boxers. "And don't." A middle finger, with that red-painted fingernail, had suddenly found its way between his cheeks, pinpointing his anus with astonishing accuracy.

"Uh, that's not for..." She smiled slyly as he found himself having difficulty speaking. He hadn't even been self-aware enough to recognize his lie, but that smile... "I mean, I've never..."

"You rule your world by day. Why not give that up, just for a night?"

Her hand departed as they entered the building and she led him to an elevator. "Shouldn't we...pay?"

"You are paying," she said, with a light tinkling of laughter. Apparently the room was included in her price. "I'd already decided to treat myself, in the hopes that I could find...a generous soul."

Once inside her hotel room, many floors up, the coat came off, and she was back in her outfit, and it must have been how her coat had fallen, but Bern could have sworn he saw her tail *flick* from one side of her to the other, like a cat's. He didn't have much time to contemplate that because she was on him with hot breath and fingers everywhere, in his hair, under his shirt scratching along his back, her hips grinding in that perfect circular way, pressing that red thong against the thick bulge in his pants. This wasn't like other conquests; he didn't really have control of it. She directed him, tearing his clothes away as they approached the bed, already covered with an odd sheet of silvery material. "Easier to clean," she explained, flicking her tongue in his ear, teasing, testing. She'd taken his cock in hand and seemed to be taking its pulse as she suggested different ideas: Directing his attention to her boots *twitch* that she kept on for him. Stroking him while taking on that disinterested façade of a perfect princess *twitch,* her other hand sliding down to where her little red thong had been *twitch* arousing herself. Slamming him down as he tried to take control *twitch* and reaching for the bedside stand, pulling out the drawer and producing, among other things, a red rope *throb.* "Oh...yes. I think you need to have control...removed." Then she paused. "You should pay me *now*."

Again, rather than finding this intrusive or rude, he respected her hustle. She'd make certain to get what she wanted, and then she'd focus on her part in completing their transaction. Of course, Lucy had also said it while pulling on fingerless leather gloves, letting him know that she'd be protecting her delicate hands from too much rough use. Bern understood then that she'd need to, that someone would be roughly used indeed.

Without reaching down, she managed to hook his pants from where they'd fallen to the floor and flip them up onto the bed. Again, Bern thought he caught motion from her tail, but it must have been the breeze from his pants landing on the bed. *She still wore that tail—did she realize how hot that made him?* He fished out his wallet and tossed it past her to the same drawer. "Can I do a fund transfer? I don't carry fifteen grand on me." He was so keyed up that even the idea of paying her seemed extraordinarily erotic to him. A way of giving himself, the best part of himself; money was his life's blood.

She accepted his smartphone to key in her account number and tapped approve herself, then set the phone down, too. Mere minutes later, Bern lay spread-eagled on the hotel bed, and that's when she produced the collar, a thin ring of black rubber that had the word SLUT written on it. "Would you be mine?" she asked him.

"Yes."

"This isn't something to take lightly. I just let you buy my time. Are you letting me purchase your body and soul?" *How did she know? How could she speak his language so well?* Bern's penis strained at the idea of being commoditized.

"Oh, please, yes!"

Lucy snapped the collar around his neck, tightly. It dug into

his neck, making him strain for each breath. Essential prelimi-
naries tended to, she sank down on top of him and slowly
unwound the red gauze from her restrained breasts. They fell
free so beautifully and for him alone. And she rode him fucking
expertly. She scratched his chest, slapped his nipples, making
them sensitive, and then bit into them. And when she gripped
him to thrust through an orgasm—she reached climax easily,
bucked and came hard, repeating in quick cycles—Lucy liked
to dig her fingers into him. He thought he caught a red glint of
blood at one point, though probably it'd just been her fingernails. Through all this he maintained a healthy hardness, but he
could feel himself closing in on a point of no return.

She hopped off him. "Oh, nuh—" he protested lamely, which
she met with unrepressed giggling.

"I didn't promise you'd get to come," she said innocently,
then looked away, ignoring him as his cock trembled, wavering
in need. She gave herself another orgasm, hovering near with
that aloof manner of the perfect girl so beyond him. After a
delighted release of her own that Bern felt as a deep ache in his
balls (and even deeper), she noticed him again. "Would you pay
extra for an orgasm?"

Oh, she was good. No, she was evil, but in such a perfect
way. He felt heat and need. "Yes, five hundred."

"Don't go cheap on something like this," she advised in a
whisper.

"A thousand!"

She set a firm hand on his cock and said, "Before I entered my
account number, I changed the transfer amount. To seventeen
thousand." His miserably aching penis returned to its fullest
hardness at this causal manipulation. "Hope that's okay."

"Two thousand more, for an orgasm," he agreed, breathless,
straining to get the words out and breath in.

Lucy launched herself back onto him, riding reverse this time, her tail whipping around to slap at him lightly. Bern threw his head back as she worked him impossibly well, using that rolling swivel as she rode his cock like none before. He felt that tail slither across him, then lift off. Her nails dug deep into his ass as she pulled at him with both hands, and then she somehow— with both hands busy, *how!?*—slipped something slick and solid up between his legs, twisting it at the last moment, finding that spot that she so easily locked on to.

Something thrust inside him. It felt...everything together... overpowering.

He gasped, somehow unable to fight against it; her hold on his cheeks pulling him apart, working with the impossible certainty of the invader. Bern didn't know much about being penetrated, but as the object forced itself into him, making him strain and suffer, his cock trembling on the verge of exploding inside her, some part of him protested that this was an impossible angle for her to penetrate him at. And her hands—both still gripping...

He lifted his head to see the visible part of her tail twitching on its own, the rest of it disappeared around her leg. No. That couldn't be. She turned her head, a viciously hungry smile on her face. The prong of her tail fucked him with increasing violence, humiliating him, yet finding a spot he never knew he had. Everything began heating up. "Yes," she hissed, as his ass enveloping the prong synchronized with the overheated pressure thumping through his cock. So fucking hot. Hot! Too hot...

"Come into me," she commanded. "Come into me now." Unable to breathe, planted deep inside her, his wrists and ankles straining against the ropes as he tried to react to her aggressive violation, he did as instructed, coming harder than a man could climax and live. More than his seed, he poured in his soul. As his body burst into flame, she bounced off, yanked the silver sheet first from one side of the bed over him, then the other. The heavy, flame-resistant material smothered the fire before his body smoked enough to set off an alarm.

Oh, she'd chosen well tonight, but then how could she go wrong these days? The greedier they were, the juicier they tasted, and the more they managed to truly satisfy. Delaying the clean-up to savor the moment just a bit longer, Lucy drifted through the room, past a couple more rolled up silver sacks, to the window, from which she could just make out Wall Street. What a beautiful view. She put a bloody finger to her lips and shuddered at the sweet taste of it. Oh, yes, it was true what they said: Greed *is* good.

STAR-CROSSED

Evan Mora

All right. Let me tell you a story. Well, actually, I don't have to tell you all of it, because most of it you already know. *Most* of it Shakespeare got right. Just not the ending, though if I'm being perfectly honest, we may have had a little something to do with that.

So here's the deal: I'm lying in the crypt, apparently dead, and Romeo is on his way to wax poetic over my corpse and kill himself with the bottle of poison he's got concealed in his cloak. Sound familiar? Yeah. I thought so. 'Course, I wasn't actually dead, though he didn't know it at the time, poor guy.

Anyway, Romeo's making his way to the crypt when— *OH!*—he gets jumped by a vampire who's intent on making a meal of him, and probably killing him in the process. I know, right? It's crazy. But Romeo's got a dagger in his cloak too, and he manages to stab this guy before he's able to drink him dry and the vampire books it out of there faster than you can say Team Edward. But he's infected, my Romeo. He's Nosferatu, the immortal undead. Which, considering he was on his way to commit suicide, really sucks. No pun intended.

Thwarted poisoning notwithstanding, Romeo still makes his way to my crypt, where he buries his head in his hands and has a good cry at the unfairness of it all. You want to talk about surprise? Imagine the look on Romeo's face when I wake up and he realizes that not only am I alive, but that he's ravenously hungry and I'm the only meal around. He shouts something about *greeting the dawn*, claps a hand over his mouth and the next thing I know he's gone, but not before I get a look at the pointy new canines he's got.

Now, Romeo is a lot of things, a lot of really, really good things. But he can be a little melodramatic and impulsive some-times, and it can really fuck things up. I mean, the solution to all of our problems just fell in his lap—he's a *vampire*, for crying out loud. All he's got to do is turn me, and voila! We're together forever, and we can leave this ridiculous family feud behind. But instead he's gone, putting that preternatural speed of his to work, and even though I spend the rest of the night running to all the places I think he might go, it becomes increasingly clear to me that I'm not going to find him before the sun lights up the eastern sky and my beloved Romeo with it. That's when the Devil shows up.

"Quite the predicament you're in," he says, amusement clear in his voice.

"Oh, sod off," I tell him angrily. Night is giving way to that early predawn gray, and in a matter of moments all that will be left of Romeo is a big pile of hot ash.

"Hey now, be nice," the Devil says. "It just so happens I'm here to offer you a solution for your problem. I know where your boy is; I can take you to him. I'll even make you an immortal myself so the two of you can spend the rest of eternity frolicking together like disgusting little love-struck bunnies." He shudders and makes a face like he's stepped in something foul.

"What's in it for you?" I ask, though really I don't care. If he can get me to Romeo before the sun incinerates him, I'll do anything he wants.

"Your soul, darling. What's *always* in it for me?" He smiles then, a wholly evil thing that would probably scare the bejeezus out of me in saner moments.

"Fine," I say, anxiously eyeing the ever-lightening sky. "Just get me to him *now!*"

"Done!" he says with a flourish and a snap of his fingers, and suddenly we're standing on the edge of a cliff next to Romeo, who's got his arms spread wide and his eyes squeezed shut, waiting for the sun to rise.

"Romeo—no!" I shout, as the first pale rays of dawn breach the horizon.

"Juliet!" he cries, extending a hand toward me.

"Oh, for Pete's sake," the Devil says with a roll of his eyes, and he snaps his fingers once more. He disappears and Romeo and I find ourselves standing in a dusty old barn where, save for a few shafts of light spilling in between the cracked and weathered boards, we're immersed in relative darkness once more.

It takes us a while to sort it all out, but when we do I wish the Devil were standing in front of me so I could send that bastard to Hell all over again myself. You see, he turned me into a life force sucking she-demon: a succubus. And my Romeo? He's got no *life force* to suck. He's the undead. But wait, it gets better. Because Romeo's a blood drinker—the hot, red, coppery kind—and whatever the black stuff is that's running through my veins now, it's no good to him; in fact, it's kind of the exact opposite of good.

And that's us in a nutshell: Romeo and Juliet, the star-crossed lovers, a pair of immortals who can't give each other the very thing necessary for their continued existence. The Devil, it seems, it not without a sense of irony.

So what's an ultrahot, sexually charged, supernatural twosome to do when faced with a predicament of this nature? Easy. Turn the twosome into a threesome...or foursome...or...well, you get the idea.

It wasn't easy in the beginning. We had issues to deal with, just like any couple that's ever been in an open relationship. Jealousy. Insecurity. Guilt. But we've had a few centuries to iron out the kinks, and I can honestly say we're stronger than ever.

Which leads me to where we are tonight: the Volcano Room, the club district's latest and greatest offering and current *it* place for all the city's young pretties. Romeo and I bypass the line outside easily enough and pass through the heavy velvet drapes into the heart of the club, where everything is bathed in blood-red light and the music pumps hypnotically from some unseen source. The space is filled to overflowing, bodies pressed tightly together, all moving to the trancelike beat. It's easily twenty degrees hotter in here than it is outside, and the room smells like sweat and perfume and too much dry ice. Sexual energy practically shimmers in the air and my hunger flares sharply as I scan the crowd, looking for something to satisfy it. A beautiful Latino boy with a chiseled body in a tight black T-shirt catches my eye, but Romeo's not sold.

"We had a boy last night," he reminds me, directing my gaze to the opposite side of the room. "What about her?"

He doesn't need to be more specific; I know exactly who he means. She's dancing alone, lost in the music, oblivious to the hungry looks directed her way. Eyes closed, head thrown back, tendrils of long dark hair clinging damply to her cheeks and her neck, her body undulates with unmistakable sensuality. Her breasts are full and firm, her belly toned and smooth where it peeks above low-rise jeans and below cropped tank top.

"Oh, yes," I say, hunger and arousal swirling deliciously together, "let's have her tonight."

The details of how we go from watching her across the room to writhing naked with her on her bed are really of little consequence. No one can resist us; that's the simple truth of it. Romeo's got his eyes and his voice—glamour, compulsion, whatever you want to call it. For me, it's all about touch. A brush of my fingertips along your forearm, a casual hand on your shoulder and you're mine. A seductive warmth steals through your limbs, a kind of euphoric bliss almost. I come on like a drug, and just that quickly, you're hooked. You'll do anything I say, go anywhere I want, just to keep it going.

She's good, this girl, the way she swirls her tongue against my clit telling me this is certainly not the first time she's gone down on another woman, and I moan my approval, stroking my hand through her long, dark hair and feeling her shuddering response to my touch. I'm propped up against the pillows at the head of her bed, she's on her knees between my thighs, and Romeo's got his hands on her hips, fucking her doggie-style.

I love watching Romeo fuck. I love the play of his muscles beneath his skin, the intense look of concentration on his face. He catches me watching him and flashes a smile; he loves watching me too. I cup my breasts together, caress them for him, roll my nipples between thumb and forefinger until they harden into tight little peaks. Something close to a growl rumbles deep in his throat, and his eyes, already dark, become nearly black.

He's fucking her harder now, driving his cock into her with all the force of his hunger and desire, and she's making these little mewling sounds of pleasure against my cunt.

"Put your tongue in my hole," I tell her. "Fuck me with your tongue."

She does what I tell her and I fist a hand in her hair, spreading my thighs even wider, fingering my clit with my free hand while her tongue plunges into me. Romeo can't take his eyes off me, and between the hunger in his gaze and this girl's tongue, my clit's so hard I'm about to explode, and I know we're on the verge of frenzy.

"You hungry, baby?" I whisper, and Romeo nods, withdrawing his cock, so I coax the girl onto her back, stroking her face, her breasts, her soft smooth belly, whispering pretty nothings to her even though she's already too lost in the pleasure coursing through her to respond.

I straddle her belly, rubbing myself against her flesh, slicking her skin with my arousal as I tease her nipples into hardness. Romeo moves into position behind me, sinking between the girl's thighs, his mouth on her sex. She's writhing and moaning, pushing up against my body, pushing closer to Romeo's mouth. She's more than ready and I'm so fucking hungry I can't wait another minute, falling over her, my hand sliding behind her neck as I fasten my mouth on hers, drawing the life force out of her in a kiss just as deadly as a vampire's.

It's bliss, pure, unadulterated bliss. Like I'm mainlining the stuff of creation, the very essence of the world, right out of this girl's mouth. Her body goes rigid, arching beneath me like a bow, and I know that Romeo's feeding too, his teeth sunk deep in her femoral artery, the combination of my kiss and his bite flooding her body with so many pleasure endorphins, it's like a never-ending orgasm crashing through her body.

I don't want it to stop, and for a moment I imagine taking everything, every bit of life from this girl's body, and a savage lust quickens within me. But that's not who we are—we figured that out a long time ago (oh, emo remorse!)—and I break away from her just as Romeo does, the girl sliding away from us into a dreamy unconsciousness, but still very much alive.

Romeo rises up in front of me, lips stained crimson, cheeks flushed with life, more darkly beautiful to me now than he had ever been in our distant human past. We come together like wild things, a fiery gnashing of teeth and tongues, the coppery taste of blood filling my mouth. Romeo throws me down on the bed, wrenching my legs apart and thrusting deeply, splitting me open, his erection hot and hard and pulsing inside me. My nails claw at his back, tearing deep furrows that heal almost instantly and he hisses, pain and pleasure both, fucking me with a violence no mortal could withstand.

With a burst of strength I turn the tables, pinning Romeo beneath me, his cock still buried deep within me. Our pace is no less frenzied than it was a moment before, but now the control is mine, and I wield it with all the skill of a true sexual demon, taking him deeper, squeezing him tighter, moving in ways that make him scream at the intensity of the pleasure rocketing through his body. And then we're there, hurtling through the void, far beyond this world and the reaches of Heaven and Hell.

The girl stirs briefly but does not wake, a testament to the heaviness of the sleep that's claimed her. I collapse on Romeo's chest, spent for now but not for long. Never, it seems, for long.

Is ours a story of woe? Hardly. (Though the tragic ending in the play was a nice touch, don't you think?) Ah, Wills...he was a fun one. We're immortal. We're in love. And anyone who ever cared a whit about whether or not we were together has been dead for hundreds of years. Stranger than fiction? Maybe. But it's the truth, and now you know what *really* became of Juliet and her Romeo.

ZACH'S
LAST RIDE

Sasha Bukova

Zach steadily twisted the throttle handle, gripping tightly as the bike zoomed like a missile across the racetrack's infield. The growl of the engine between his legs drowned out the cheers of the surrounding fans, but the beer-guzzling mob in the grandstand was the last thing on Zach's mind. His attention instead focused on the bright-blue ramp that loomed in his path. As he roared up the incline and shot into space, he felt the familiar rush that accompanied his stunts. From his chest, to his gut, to his balls, the sensation of flying felt like an orgasm spurred on by fuel instead of flesh.

Indeed, those few airborne seconds were blissful. He was oblivious to the twenty-five buses lined up side to side below him or the flashbulbs exploding in the stands on all sides. He only wanted to stay in the sky, to hurtle through space like a bullet. The mixture of speed and danger felt like a potent, fleeting cocktail.

All too soon, the landing ramp approached. He hit the

steel ramp with a thud, his bike coasting down to the far end of the infield with plenty of room to spare. He stopped with a dramatic skid, waving to the crowd and bowing slightly. He got off the bike and walked with long, slow strides to the opposite side. Some college-age girls in the front row held up a paper banner proclaiming ZACH RYDER ROCKS in big block letters. The girls eyed his muscular body, clearly pleased by the way his red, white and blue leather pants and jacket hugged his legs, torso and bulging crotch. Typical summer night at the Southern Indiana County Raceway, he thought, where the entire population of the small farm town turned out to watch the great Ryder take another jump over a fleet of vehicles. Last week he'd jumped over a row of tractors in Duncan, Iowa. Two weeks before, it was monster trucks in Bakersfield, California. As he waved, he kept the visor over his face. He didn't want people to see the post-jump excitement fading from his eyes.

A gaggle of local dignitaries—the mayor, his daughter, the local beauty queen—awaited him on the edge of the infield, but Zach only gave a few cursory handshakes before breaking off from the crowd and heading toward the stadium's exit. As the rush from the jump faded, Zach always wanted to be alone. It wasn't a secret: his handlers knew not to disturb him in these moments as he trudged to his trailer.

He entered the long Airstream and threw his helmet onto a table cluttered with insurance paperwork. He ambled to the back of the trailer and settled into a swivel chair situated in front of a full-length mirror, his tired blue eyes staring back at him. Throughout his life, those eyes had seen sights that most men would never dream of. He'd trekked across otherworldly landscapes from Africa to Alaska in cross-country motorcycle races. He'd spent crazy, lust-filled nights with world-famous models and A-list actresses. He'd snorted coke with Super Bowl champions, poured insanely expensive champagne on half-naked revelers during Mardi Gras.

But as he looked at his reflection, he realized something was missing. He still wanted more. His appetite for excitement seemed inexhaustible. Where would he find satisfaction?

Something in the reflection caught his gaze. It was a woman standing in the shadows behind him. She wore a skintight leather body suit that clung to her legs, hips and waist like a second skin. Her ample tits strained against her top, which was unzipped low enough to reveal the deep cleft between them. The long, black hair that spilled across her shoulders framed an oval face of fair, porcelain-clear skin. Full lips painted black parted slightly, violet eyes burned with dark fire.

Zach shook his head. "Happens every time. You tell security not to let anyone in, and they open the door to any girl who bats her eyelashes," he said.

"On the contrary, they never even noticed me," she said with clear, crisp pronunciation. "I slipped right past."

"Oh, so you can turn invisible, right?" he asked.

"I have my ways."

"Well, I wish we could chat," he said. "But groupie time is over."

"I'm not a groupie," she said.

"That's what they all say," said Zach, punching in the three-digit security number. "Let me guess: You're my soul mate. My number-one fan. A motorcycle journalist who just wants an interview. Well, whoever you are, you're not on my schedule."

"I'm here to help you get what you want," she said.

"And that is?" He held the phone to his ear.

"You want a real rush," she said. "These motorcycle stunts are fine, but they're over too quickly, aren't they?"

Zach hung up the phone and spun the chair around to face her.

"You feel an emptiness that gnaws at you," she said. "You want a much, much, bigger high, but you don't believe it exists."

He felt as if she'd peered into his mind, and the awareness unsettled him. He stood up and drew closer to her. A honey-suckle-sweet scent rose from her hair. Her lips were wet and parted. He felt the stirrings of arousal in his crotch.

"So you're a psychic, huh?" he asked. "Just like that gypsy lady who works a booth at the fairgrounds. Tell me, what other secrets do you have?"

"What does it matter?" she asked. "The only important thing is the thrill you're hunting. The big game."

"Maybe you've got me all wrong," he said. "Maybe I'm done with the stunts. Maybe I'm going to give it up tomorrow, pack it all in and settle up in Wyoming. Find a nice stream to hunker down next to and prop up my fishing pole."

"I don't think so," she said. Her hand found his crotch and pressed against his member. Her slim palm rubbed in soft, up-and-down motions on the white leather. The touch was perfect, gentle enough to glide smoothly across the trousers, hard enough to stimulate the throbbing flesh between his legs. His hardening manhood strained against the cow skin.

He looked into her eyes. Two pools of violet that seemed to hide a multitude of secrets. What did she know about him? And how did she know it?

"I'm not like that cornfield beauty queen you fucked at the last state fair," she said. "Or that bleach-blonde swimsuit model you banged in the truck bed outside the splash tank."

"How could you know—?"

"Oh, those sluts were pretty enough. And their pussies were

plenty wet and tight. But I don't think that tiara holder even climaxed. All the work she put into shaving her sweet cooch? What good is it if she can't even enjoy it?"

"You've been following me," he said. "Spying on me."

"And that swimsuit model must have been a disappointment for you. It's a bit of a turn off when spray tan rubs off on you while doing doggie-style, isn't it?"

"You're a stalker," he said.

She shook her head. "Stalkers are delusional. They have no grasp of reality. I *am* reality."

"You're crazy," he said.

"You know I'm real." It was true. He felt the power flow through her fingers like an electric current. Behind her pretty face lay a force that couldn't be denied. He wanted to taste more.

"So what do you want?" he asked.

"I want to take you to the edge," she said. "And I know you want to go there so bad that it aches." She uttered the last word with a hard squeeze of her hand. He felt desire course through his body. Her caresses grew more fervent, and he felt on the brink of orgasm.

"You think that feels good? You just wait."

She took a step back. He wanted to reach out, tear that leather off of her body, but something warned him to stay his hand. She turned toward the door.

"Where are you going?" he asked.

"I'll be back," she said, and walked out the door. He fought the temptation to run after her, but stopped in his tracks. He knew she'd return.

Days passed. Zach went from state fair to state fair, dazzling crowds with his spectacular jumps, returning to his trailer to stare into the mirror again, wondering when she'd return. Sleep came fitfully, and often he'd hear her voice promising to take him to new heights of ecstasy.

Then, on a muggy night at a fairground near Omaha, he was awakened by the howl of a motorcycle engine roaring outside of his trailer. Dressed only in shorts, he emerged into a warm night lit by a full moon. She sat on an idling bike just outside the Airstream, her shapely body clad only in a leather tube top, boots and skimpy black shorts. The grumbling custom bike looked as if it was designed by a madman: all big engine and wide tires with high, wide handlebars that resembled devil's horns. She smiled and then burned rubber, darting off into the night like a phantom. Zach ran to his bike and hit the throttle, pouring all of his skill into pursuing her through dusty farm roads that threaded endless cornfields. Keeping up wasn't easy. Her souped-up hog pushed her to ungodly speeds, and she navigated tight turns as if riding a much nimbler bike. Still, he kept her in his view, drinking in the shape of her delectable ass as he pursued her, the dry summer wind whipping his naked torso.

Just when he thought he'd lost her in the darkness, he spied a light in the distance. As he drew closer he saw a barn silhouetted against the night sky with a lone ray of light peeking out of a half-opened door. He recognized the unmistakable shape of her grotesquely brawny bike parked out front. He parked his motorcycle and peeked through the door.

The inside looked nothing like a barn. Instead, it was a shrine to riding. Leather jackets, racing banners, gloves, boots and other biker gear hung on the walls like trophies. Instead of animal stalls, the barn's floor was strewn with sculptures made out of grotesquely twisted and bent motorcycle frames. Some were festooned with skulls, others adorned with gaudy reflectors and turning lights.

His gaze quickly shifted to the bed that sat on the other side of the massive space.

It was made almost completely of motorcycle parts. Exhaust pipes welded end to end constituted the bed's four posts. Racing leather was sewn together to make a crude canopy. The headboard was a collage of headlights, rims and spokes. Candles surrounding the bed cast a sensual glow around the tableau.

And lying naked on the bed amid a pile of leather cushions was the girl. Her head reclined on a pillow, hair spilling out in long, luscious strands. Her exposed breasts swelled into two voluptuous mounds topped by pink, erect nipples. Her long legs stretched enticingly along the bed, two flesh highways converging on a small, enticing tuft of hair.

"Took you long enough," she said.

He walked toward her, shedding his shorts to free his erection. "I don't even know your name," he said. "Who are you?"

Her lips moved, but the blood pumping in his ears blocked out the sound. He knelt at the foot of the bed, kissing her milky-white thighs and licking the salty skin, leaving a wet saliva trail to her pussy. His mouth reached the promised land, the sweet, flowing juices tasting like ambrosia on his grateful lips. He slid his eager tongue along the slit of her pussy, parting her succulent lips, probing her hot, wet hole. His hands reached up and spread her wide and her fully exposed clit swelled in greeting. He eagerly licked and sucked the bud, his tongue lashing her with rapid, frenetic caresses. Her back arched to his attention, her body vibrating to the moans that issued from her parted mouth. Through the haze of his desire, he heard her murmur a string of words in a foreign language, an incantation recited through excited breaths. The spell only excited him more—he felt his cock throb with almost unbearable hardness.

Mouth glistening with her juices, he rose to his feet, his long, thick dick pulsing hard in the warm air. She stroked it, long delicate fingers savoring every contour.

"Lie down and close your eyes" she whispered, her eyes flashing with mischief in the candlelight.

He complied and let the bed absorb his long, muscular body. The cushions yielded to his back like the finest down, but the sensations of comfort were dwarfed by the thrills she dished out with her lips and tongue. She started at his mouth—deep, wet kisses, tongues pushing and twisting. He ran his hands along her back and ass. Her body was equal parts athlete and vixen: toned, taut muscles and to-die-for curves. His cock felt starved for her pussy.

She covered his torso in kisses, licking, sucking and biting his nipples. She dragged her long tongue along his stomach, lingering on his naval. She took her time licking up and down the length of his engorged shaft, licking the cleft of his ball sac, mixing his ample precum with her spit before slowly wrapping her full lips around his raging cock and swallowing him all the way to the root.

She bobbed her head slowly at first, then quickened the pace, her warm, wet mouth pleasuring his hungry member. He peeked to watch, and for a moment their eyes locked. He fought the urge to cum as he gazed at the strange fire that blazed in her violet eyes. Something beastly, something demonic burned there. Instead of repelling him, the gaze only heightened his arousal. He grunted uncontrollably in excitement, a nakedly primal thrill running through his body.

Lifting her head, she said, "You're ready," crawling back to him on all fours.

"Please," he said. "Take me to the edge."

With the grace of a dancer, she straddled him and then impaled herself on his rock-hard member, slowly engulfing the throbbing cock in her pussy. Her slippery hole tightly embraced him, the pleasure growing as she took him in, inch by inch. She began moving, first gently rocking her hips, then riding him hard up and down, dangling her breasts over his lips to suck and lick. He gripped her hips, guiding her, holding on to her, fingers squeezing soft skin. Head thrown back, she resumed her mad incantations, the words flying out of her mouth as if escaping by their own accord.

He felt as if he'd explode at any minute, but somehow he held on. He opened his eyes again and gasped at the sight that greeted him. The walls of the barn had disappeared. In their place, a starry night sky stretched into infinity. Tongues of purple flame shot up along the foot and sides of the bed, a fiery halo that threw off a wicked heat. *This must be a hallucination,* he thought—but she hadn't given him any drug. The bed rolled and pitched, and he feared he'd be thrown into space to plummet into an endless void. He dug his fingers into the fabric for purchase.

"No!" she said, the fire in her eyes blazing with even greater intensity. "Let go! Free yourself!"

He released his grip, realizing in that moment that she was delivering him exactly what he wanted: sexual ecstasy mingled with harrowing danger. The elixir sent him to a new plane of excitement.

Together, they flew through the emptiness, fucking with a frenzied intensity until they came in tandem. Their shared climax lasted for what seemed like hours—waves and waves of pleasure coursed through his body. He opened his eyes again and saw a white light streaming out of his torso like a slow-motion electric current. The liquid radiance poured into her mouth, and she drank it greedily. In the throes of ecstasy, he was powerless to stop her from devouring his essence. Indeed, in those last spasms of his peak, he realized who she was. He faded from consciousness, the sensations of pleasure replaced by the feeling of plummeting into infinite darkness.

The deputy grimaced as he spoke into his shoulder radio. The midday sun beat down on him like a hot stove. "Yes, we've located Ryder. But he's in a bad way."

"Is he injured?" said the dispatcher through static.

"Not physically. We found him sitting outside of this old, abandoned barn, naked and spaced out," the sheriff said, taking off his wide-brimmed hat and fanning his sweating forehead. "A weird, goofy smile was plastered on the fella's face."

"Any sign of his bike?"

"No. But there's a few parts here and there on the ground: a kickstand, a brake handle. Looks like the motorcycle was stripped and hauled off."

Suddenly, the daredevil's lips moved. The sheriff strode to the squad car where Zach sat wrapped in a blanket in the backseat, his glazed eyes staring into space and his lips moving.

The sheriff put his ear close to Zach's mouth, only to hear the same thing whispered over and over again.

"I'm never coming down. Never coming down."

DELIVERANCE

Jay Lawrence

The young man had been a long time traveling through the seemingly endless forest. The fir trees looked as if they were huddling together for warmth in the stillness of the December days. And the days were short, so he rose as soon as the pallid winter sun appeared above the horizon, and made camp when it slid beneath the mountains in a fiery glow. He traveled on foot, his stout boots crunching a regular rhythm in the crisp light snow. At night, the sound of distant wolves made his heart beat faster and he stoked his campfire and fingered the long knife that was his only protection. Each day his pack became lighter as he used up his provisions, but it only seemed to grow more burdensome. The bright lights and gay amusements of the city were far behind, as if in another world.

His fingers and toes were lightly frostbitten, his hair a wild and tangled mass and he had not shaved since leaving home a week before. He spurred himself on, like an ailing horse, with thoughts of hot roast pheasant and wine. He could almost taste the rich succulent flesh of the fowl as he marched on through the gloom. He imagined tearing it apart with his aching fingers, relishing the savory oily juice that would coat his desiccated lips. The claret would warm his throat from tongue to belly. On and on he stumbled, because there was no turning back. He had a message to deliver.

On the afternoon of the eighth day, he came upon a beautiful but sadly neglected house. It was perched upon a vast granite outcrop, facing the setting sun, and almost seemed to grow out of its rocky foundation, as if it were one with the harsh terrain. The young man wandered about the deserted mansion's grounds, growing vaguely uneasy as he sensed that he was observed by hidden eyes. Yet every time he glanced up at the windows of the desolate hall, all that could be seen was the dusty darkness within. He fingered the knife, stroked its razor-sharp edge. It was getting dark again and he was so desperately *cold*. The young man decided that, ghosts or no ghosts, he would find a way into the sad old house, make a fire in the grate and have shelter for the night. The sun was setting as he kicked against a crumbling door, its distant wintry rays reddening the windows of the hall as if there was a fire within.

It's so beautiful.

He was in a vast chamber with a great fireplace. The lofty walls were draped with ancient moldering tapestries. The glass-eyed heads of stuffed and mounted game peered blindly into the echoing space. A long table of dark, almost black wood took pride of place in the once magnificent room. On the table, as if recently abandoned, stood an empty wineglass. Somehow the sight of the glass instilled a deep melancholy in him, a peculiarly irrational sadness that seemed to have crept like an insidious miasma from the very fabric of the house.

What nonsense. I must be more tired than I thought.

Shaking himself like a dog just out of water, the young man set to making a modest fire in the grate. He unpacked his meager supper of dry bread and sausage and set to toasting it over the flames, whistling softly to himself, and shivering as the small blaze thawed his well-chilled limbs. He'd never felt such cold. It seemed to insinuate itself into the very marrow of his bones, despite his stout clothes. Huddled on a sheepskin rug, the young man fell asleep, thankful for one night in which he would not have to keep an ear open for the wolves.

Sometime in the dark depths of the freezing night, he woke with a start, as if a sudden sound had roused him from his dreams. The house was silent but, to his amazement, the fire in the grate had not died down to embers as he slept. Indeed, a gay conflagration danced in the fireplace. The young man stared at the leaping flames and his heart skipped a beat. Someone had put some logs on the fire. This was not the mean little blaze of sticks and twigs over which he had toasted his bread. A soft sound from the other side of the chamber made him whirl around. There was a rustle of skirts as a small slender figure emerged from a shadowy corner.

"Good evening, Christian."

The voice belonged to a young woman in a deep blue gown.

The young man was horrified. But the house was empty! It seemed he had made a terrible mistake and deserved to be thrown out into the frigid night. And how did she know his name? It was his given name, the one no one ever used, preferring a trite nickname. Had she looked through his belongings to ascertain the identity of her intruder? Christian stumbled to his feet.

"Madam, please forgive my inexcusable behavior! I truly believed this house was abandoned and sought shelter from the cold."

The young woman smiled graciously.

"I understand. My home is not what it once was. Please do not distress yourself. Are you hungry?"

Christian thought of his pathetic meal of sausage and bread.

"I have eaten, but not well. But please do not go to any trouble on my behalf. Under the circumstances…"

The young woman placed a delicate finger against her rosebud lips.

"Hush now. I'm fond of eating late at this time of year. You cannot travel on with a half-empty belly."

Christian could not disagree. What marvelous good fortune! It was odd that the lady did not appear frightened by his impromptu appearance by her fireside, but he was glad that it was so. He warmed his back by the crackling fire as he watched her set the table. Then she disappeared to some other chamber to procure their meal. Within a few minutes, she returned, bearing a laden tray, which the young man carried to the table.

"I hope you like pheasant. And there is a nice claret. I drink so little by myself, it's a treat to have company."

Christian stared at the delicious food that was neatly arrayed on a silver platter. It was the supper of his daydream in the frozen forest. Perhaps he was hallucinating. Slyly, he pinched himself on one thigh but the sensation seemed real enough.

"You are very kind, Miss…?"

The young woman frowned slightly.

"You may call me Delphine. Now please…eat! It really would give me such pleasure to see you well fed."

Christian ate. Everything was superb. The pheasant was meltingly tender and full of fragrant herb-scented juice, the accompanying root vegetables were sweet and faintly caramelized by roasting around the bird. The wine was excellent, as soft

and round as a lovely woman's thighs. After recharging his plate
and glass several times, he finally sat back in his chair, feeling
more content than he could ever recall. In his haste to eat and
drink, he had paid little attention to his lovely companion and,
realizing his folly, he flushed deeply and muttered his contrition
into his napkin.

"It seems I must make my apologies once again. I make a
poor dining companion."

The young woman shrugged.

"A better companion than spiders and moths. I do so yearn
for human contact."

At last, Christian examined his hostess's features. She was
very pale, with fine golden hair neatly parted down the middle
of her scalp then swept back into a softly gleaming coil. Her
eyes were an indeterminate gray blue, the kind of shade that
changes with the light. There was a translucency about her, a
delicate porcelain doll effect.

*Yet she must be as strong as iron to survive alone in this
desolate place.*

Assorted questions sprang into Christian's mind, lingered
briefly then were dismissed.

She's so lovely.

Suddenly, his head reeled with the rich food, the wine and the
heat of the blazing fire. His blood beat in his ears and every inch
of his body seemed suffused with heat after the interminable
chill. He was vaguely aware of his hostess taking his hand. She
spoke as softly as snow falling on snow.

"Do you want to kiss me?"

He didn't pause to consider her question but merely nodded
and answered, "Yes." Surely she was mesmerizing him. It was
a terrible impropriety, but he did not care. Who would see or
know? His mouth found hers and he kissed the dainty rosebud

lips that tasted of wine and pheasant and something else that he could not quite discern. She was wonderfully giving yet yielding and, again, Christian imagined her as a doll. In his passion, he imagined doing with her exactly as he desired, yet, in truth, he had little experience of the fairer sex.

"Take me as the wolves converge upon their prey, as the eagle swoops to spear a fish."

She had read his mind. Indeed, it seemed as if she was within his mind. Moaning with desire, Christian pressed his lips upon the sweet clean skin of the young woman's throat. Something in him wanted to bite, nip, suck. He had become a predator and Delphine was willing prey. The next moment, her tiny fingers felt like steel rods in his hair, twisting and drawing his head to her half-exposed bosom. With one harsh movement, he wrenched the flimsy bodice of her dress aside and revealed her lovely ivory breasts. Again, she pushed his face toward her succulence, crying for him to feast upon her. Christian drew his mouth over the perfect mounds of satiny flesh, which reminded him strongly of two neatly molded milk puddings, sweet and creamy, wobbling on the spoon of his tongue. Delphine's nipples were pale pink sweetmeats, berry shaped and swollen, and he drew them into his mouth one by one, sucking hard, causing his hostess to shriek. He thought of her moist little cunny. It would be honey—manna to lap until she passed out with pleasure. His rod was harder than it had ever been, pressing against his trousers like a caged animal.

"Devour me. Make me yours!"

There was no sense of time's passing as the feverish young man entered his partner. She felt like burning velvet as her hot cushioned passage swallowed him whole to the hilt and seemed to search for more. His fat knob met the resistance of her womb and knocked insistently, his hips grinding and bucking in a wild primeval rhythm. No one had taught him the dance and its frenzied, abandoned steps were far from the clumsy fumblings of his few past affairs. Delphine began to scream and to tear at his hair as he erupted within her depths, feeling as if every last drop of his essence had left him to become part of her.

He must have fallen asleep as swiftly as a babe does. The pale morning sun cast feeble fingers of light through the dusty windows of the old house as the young man stirred. The fire was long dead in the grate and his bones ached from stiffness and chill. Slowly, Christian got to his feet, looking sleepily about him for signs of the lovely young woman. She must have retired to her chamber, wherever that was. Oddly, everything seemed strangely unmarked by their midnight tumbling. He could even see his own footprints in the heavy dust that carpeted the floor of the ancient hall, *but not hers*. A shiver ran down his spine, one that was not caused by the terrible cold. Hallucination? Dream? He would not think about it. He would dismiss it from his mind. Briskly, he collected his pack and left the house, horribly aware of the single dust-drenched glass that still sat on the long, ebony table. Outside, the snow was falling, as soft as the feathers in a maiden's powder puff. Two more days and, God willing, he'd deliver the message and be done with the ordeal.

Into the forest again he strode, knowing full well she watched him from a window above, but not looking back, else he be turned to ice with the horror of what he saw.

MINIONS HAVE NEEDS TOO

Anya Richards

The hunt was successful?"

Keeping her gaze lowered, Syllabelle shivered, the energy trapped inside writhing, firing her blood anew.

"Yes, master," she whispered, longing to look up. It had been so long since she'd been in his presence the urge to devour him with her gaze was almost too strong to overcome. "I hope to please you."

"We shall see." Theodictus's voice rasped over her skin like the rough tongue of a cat, causing her to tremble even more, need twisting deep in her belly.

Chancing his annoyance, she shuffled a little closer on her knees until his strong bare feet came into her line of sight. "All I desire is your approval."

Theodictus laughed, a boom of sound that ricocheted through her bones and made yearning flare and pop through her body. Her breasts ached and her cunt throbbed in time with his mirth.

"Is it, sweetling?" His feet shifted, moved farther apart, toes curling slightly into the smooth stone floor. "Is there nothing else you want from your master?"

The mocking tone, the hint of cruelty, caused fear to blossom cold in her belly, but also heightened her need.

Careful, she told herself, *careful*.

"I also desire your pleasure, and if it should please you to send me away..."

He was silent for so long fear turned to terror, and she envisioned once more being sent to the incubi who, in greed and desperation, would carelessly suck her carefully collected tribute away. The thought almost made her beg, plead, but that would only make it worse. So, instead, she chose meek stillness, holding her breath as she waited.

Finally, when she could hardly bear the quietude a moment longer, Theodictus chuckled.

"Convince me it is worth my while to receive what you have brought. If it pleases me, I will take what you have to give. Tell me of the hunt."

Relief stole her breath, and she was forced to inhale deeply, taking in the scent of his expensive cologne; the elusive, under-lying hint of brimstone; before she could reply.

"Would it please you, master, to see it instead?"

She heard his hissed breath, the rush of movement as he sat forward, and inwardly smiled. Theodictus was her master, but she knew him well. Her skill at retaining the remnants of her hunts, the ability to hold and transmit them, was unusual among her kind. It raised her value and, although she knew it would never be enough to keep her completely safe, she'd honed it during her banishment.

"You've worked hard, little one, to regain my favor." The harsh gruffness of his words filled her with pride, but she tamped it down, for just such an emotion had led to her previous punishment. The centuries spent slowly starved of sustenance, and then being mauled by the incubi, had taught a painful lesson.

"Yes, master."

Again silence, but now it hung heavy, like a humid pall laced with arousal between them. Suddenly his leg moved, one foot coming to rest against her knee.

"Show me what you have for me."

The breath she took shuddered into her lungs and, as she reached out a trembling hand to caress his foot, she released one memory—

He was the lookout in an alley, the drug dealer's boy, a hard case scrabbling up the twisted ladder of his chosen profession, unafraid and always ready for the worst. Around him bubbled an aura so black and angry it washed like acid over Syllabelle's skin.

Turning, he saw her coming into the moonlight, reached instinctively for his gun. Then the fact of her unarmed nakedness broke through, and he smiled.

By then she was close enough to cup his cheeks, capture his glittering gaze with hers.

"You are mine," she whispered. "All mine."

He struggled, unwilling to submit, to bow to anyone. But she had him, refused to release her hold, and when she took his lips he surrendered all at once, flooding her with his desperate, angry desire.

Pushing him against the wall, she undid the heavy belt buckle, unfastened his jeans. He pushed the pants down, low growls of need pulsing from his throat and into her mouth.

"Be still now," she whispered, delving deep into his psyche, finding the one moment in his life he never, ever wanted to let go—pulling him back into it. "Be still, and come with me."

"Oh, geez, Cindy." His voice was suddenly so young, and he was once more looking down at the sweet-faced blonde kneeling between his trembling legs. She'd left her tank top pulled up so her creamy breasts swung free, the nipples tight and wet with his saliva. Her Cupid's bow mouth was slightly open, glistening from his kisses. "You don't have to."

The tip of her tongue peeked out from between innocently curved lips, and he groaned.

"I want to." Her eyes were so blue they could have been shards of a summer sky. "I have to taste you. I've wanted to for so long."

Around them in the dank basement lay the remnants of his poverty-stricken life—a sofa so moldy he wouldn't even let her sit on it, the boxes his old man had tossed down the stairs and forgotten. But as the warm, succulent mouth touched his cock for the first time, and her tongue slicked a silken path around the head, he was suddenly richer than any other man in the world.

Drawing back, eyelids heavy with passion, she smiled, and his heart slammed with happiness. "You taste so good, baby." She licked her lips again, and his balls tightened to the point of pain. "I love the shape of your cock, how hard and soft it is, all at the same time."

"Don't Cindy." He could hardly speak, already hovering on the edge of coming just from hearing those words from her sweet lips. "Don't talk like that."

In reply she licked a path of warm fire down to his sac and back up again. "Why not, hm?"

The last part of her question was hummed around the head of his dick, and he stiffened, pushed her gently away, almost dying from the suction she kept on him right until he was released.

"You'll make me come, Cindy."

"*I want you to.*" *Soft fingers touched his balls, and her breath puffed against his aching flesh. "I want to watch you blow your wad.*"

"*Cindy.*" *The word wheezed from his throat, and she giggled softly, palming his cock, wrapping her fingers around it, pumping.*

"*I wish we could fuck,*" *she whispered, "and I could feel you inside me. I want to spread my legs and let you look at my pussy, suck on it the way you suck my tits, until I'm screaming and begging you to take me.*"

All he could do was groan, imagining it, feeling the wet heat of her virgin cunt surrounding him, milking him as she screamed his name, her ass flailing under him, his balls slamming against her.

"*Fuck,*" *he shouted, as she took him deep into her throat. Fantasy merged with reality, and he pumped into that innocent, fucking* incredible *mouth, the come shooting out of him like bullets from an automatic weapon...*

Shuddering from the transfer of memory, reliving the orgasm she'd had while stealing the oblivious drug dealer's seed, energy and memory, Syllabelle stroked the burning hot flesh beneath her fingers. Theodictus's harsh breathing echoed through the chamber, each rasp of sound filling her with delight.

"A hard man returned to the most innocent and thrilling sexual experience of his life." The demon's voice was soft, just a rumble of sound. "Intriguing, Syllabelle."

He withdrew his foot, and she felt the loss like a blow.

"Did it please you, master?"

She hadn't meant to ask, for to show Theodictus any weakness was to court disaster, but the words emerged before she could stop them. For a long moment he didn't answer, but then his feet shifted farther apart.

"It is good." There was no mistaking the lust coloring his words. "I will take your tribute."

"There is more, master."

A growl of pleasure, quickly curtailed, broke from his chest, but he couldn't hide his eagerness as he said, "Another? Give it to me." Grasping her hair, he pulled her forward, so her lips were a hair's breadth from his cock. "What else do you have for me, Syllabelle? I want to know."

The thick rasp of his voice betrayed his excitement, and triumph struck fire through her veins as she leaned to take his cock deep into her mouth and release the memory...

She made him chase her, never staying in one section of the club long enough for him to make his move. The hunter was actually the hunted, although he would never acknowledge such a thing as possible.

Flaunting his body on the dance floor, he rolled his hips in perfect time to the music, pretending not to see the way the women watched, the interest and desire etched on their faces.

After teasing him, keeping him running for an hour or more, Syllabelle let him catch her gaze, give her one of his long, lust-inducing stares. She pouted slightly, as if deliberating whether to encourage him or not, and then turned away, heading for the exit.

By the time she had turned into the alley running alongside the building he was coming behind her, his arousal and anger reaching to envelop her. One hand closed over her breast while the other fastened around her throat.

"Glad you waited for me, bitch."

She laughed as she twisted and swung around to immobilize him in an arm-lock. Before he knew what was happening, he was on his knees. Twisting her fingers into his hair, Syllabelle yanked his head back, forcing him to look up at her as she loomed behind him.

"Glad you could make it, asshole."

"What the fu—?"

But she had him, was already inside him, scouring his brain, holding him in thrall. She released his arm and it fell, limp, to his side. She retained the punishing grip on his hair.

"What were you going to do, Gavin? Tell me, now."

"Fuck you up against the wall, from behind." His voice was thick, and tears gathered in the corners of his eyes. "Give it to you good."

"Really?" She touched his throat above the Adam's apple, giving him a taste of her power—just a sharp jolt—enough to make him whimper and tremble. "You don't know how to give it to a woman good, Gav, but I think I'd like to teach you." He whimpered again, a pleading sound, and she laughed softly. "Are you hard, little man?"

He had to tell the truth—had no choice with her power driving into him like spikes.

His eyes were stretched wide, his mouth worked to get the single word out. "Yes."

She stepped around him, still grasping his hair, laughed again at the sight of a tear escaping to trail down his cheek.

"Do you suck pussy, Gav?"

Her scorn made him flinch. "No, never," he whispered. "I don't have to do that kind of thing to get a woman hot."

"So, you like your women hot?" Stepping forward put her crotch right in front of his chin. "And you think your ridiculous, deviant self enough to achieve that?" A little more power made his eyes roll back. A hard tug on his hair refocused his attention on her face. "Stick out your tongue, worm."

There was no hesitation in his response, and she lifted her skirt, straddling his face, sliding her hell-hot pussy over his tongue, riding his mouth, letting the dominance pull her closer and closer to orgasm.

When she drew away he tried to follow, but her punishing grip kept him still.

With a flick of her wrist, she threw him onto his back and bent to shred his pants. In moments he lay naked from the waist down and moaning, cock standing straight up, the head purple, precome drizzling down the length. Stepping forward, she planted one foot beside his chest, the other so the heel of her stiletto rested on the bundle of nerves at the base of his pectoral muscle. His mouth opened on a soundless wail, and she smiled, lifted her skirt.

"You can't satisfy me, Gav." She parted the lips of her pussy, slicked a finger around her clitoris. "Any woman who's with you will have to take care of herself."

He gulped, tried to speak, but he was riveted on her fingers, now sliding into her cunt, gliding smoothly in and out. Tilting her hips, she brought herself to a hard, fast orgasm, moaning and mewling to torment him further.

Looking down into his glazed eyes, she backed away. Hooking the toe of her shoe under first one of his legs and then the other, she forced them up until they curled against his chest. His vulnerable position aroused her anew.

Turning, she squatted over his hips and roughly brought his cock into position. It was cool in comparison to her heat, and she felt his silent howl of pain, his instinctive attempt to thrust into her despite the agony. Laughing, she engulfed him, taking him deep, just as she plunged a finger into his arse, making him erupt, his screams echoing in her ears, joining her shout of satisfaction...

Theodictus shuddered, his cock pulsating with a primal

rhythm in her throat.

"You minx," he growled, holding her head, pushing deeper. "You know I love a revenge fuck."

Syllabelle moaned her agreement, rubbing her tongue against the hard, silken flesh. The barriers of his power slipped beneath the onslaught of her gift, tempting her to test their strength, but she held back, let the cracks remain unexplored.

The fingers entwined in her hair yanked with brutal upward force and she was suddenly standing. Theodictus's fiery gaze held hers as he bared his strong, white teeth in a parody of a smile.

"You have pleased me." He tried to make it a gift, but she could see his greed and want. "I will take your tribute."

Tugging her forward, he made her straddle his massive thighs. Fingers digging into her hips, he forced her down, thrusting up at the same time so he filled and stretched her completely. Holding on to the corded muscles of his shoulders, she rode his cock with long, fast strokes.

"Yes." He closed his eyes, began to take the tribute, the rough suction of the transfer almost taking her to orgasm. "Give it to me."

So she did—flooding him all at once with stored-up memories, creating a devastating wave of stimulation and culmination. He shuddered with ecstasy, not realizing the cracks in his dominance were turning to fissures, showing the way to his essence, the dark heart of his being.

With a cry of intense pleasure she latched on to it, still riding his thrusting, pulsing cock, gorging on the thick, intoxicating power. Theodictus bellowed, finally tried to break free, but it was too late. Syllabelle was already taking far more than she gave, sucking him dry, growing stronger until he had no choice but to keep fucking and fucking, howling in tandem with her shrieks of triumph.

"No," he screamed. "What have you done?"

Gripping his face, she looked deep into his eyes, the horror there enough to make her grin. "Give me the last of it, Theodictus. It is time."

His mouth worked, but no words came and she saw the exact, devastating moment he realized what was about to happen.

With a strangled cry of outrage at the inescapable bliss, he came, flooding her with the seed of hundreds, thousands of human men, tainted now with the remnants of his authority. It was almost the last of what he was, and he released it, unable to stop. Drained in every possible way, Theodictus's form grew limp, and Syllabelle climbed off his lap to stand for a moment looking down at him. Although physically the same, his aura of command was gone, leaving him diminished. Slumped in the ornate chair he so loved, eyes closed as though unwilling to open and see the evidence of his fall.

"How?" he whispered.

She laughed lightly, saw his eyelids flicker. "I'm not sure, but I must thank you for it. Brutes though the incubi may be, it was being forced to service them that showed me it was possible. Releasing memories to them weakened their natural defenses against my taking their essences. If it was possible with them, wouldn't it be with you? So I stored memories, knowing it would take many to overcome your power."

He didn't reply, but stepped down from the throne to kneel at her feet, head bowed in supplication.

"Mistress."

The word filled her with a rush of need, but she ignored it. Beautiful Theodictus, the creator of her existence, would always be a danger. In a millennium or so he might regain his power—through connivance or unforeseen happenstance—and she couldn't risk keeping him in her realm.

But there was time enough to enjoy the moment, savor the heady knowledge of having her first minion. Stepping around him, she took her place on the throne, and spread her legs wide.

"Theodictus," she said softly, aware that even they who serve have feelings. "Please me."

Hatred, fear and desire burned in his gaze but, obedient, he covered her pussy with his mouth, wicked tongue dancing over her aroused and sensitized flesh. Curling fingers into his midnight locks, she tugged him closer, ground against his face. With thighs closing tight around his head she began to feed, surprised at how much life force he still possessed. The rumble of Theodictus's moan pushed her to ecstasy.

Perhaps she would keep him for a century or so.

Good minions were so hard to find.

SWEET TOOTH

Nan Andrews

Shelly set a box of utensils on the kitchen counter. Paula followed her into the kitchen with her arms full. "You sure have a lot of glasses. What happened to the pots and pans?"

"You know me, I like to drink, not cook."

"Yeah, I know. Speaking of which, when's the housewarming party going to be?"

"Give me a few weeks to unpack, please." Shelly had walked past the old Victorian house every day for two years on her way to work. One cold November morning, she noticed a For Rent sign in the window and immediately called the number. The manager showed her the apartment that afternoon and she took it. The house had originally been a single-family home. Her first floor apartment had been a parlor, the formal dining room and the kitchen. Now it was a studio of sorts, with the parlor and dining room making one big space, and a newer bathroom stuck between it and the kitchen. Shelly loved the old cabinets and the checked linoleum in the kitchen, even though she didn't plan to use it much.

She opened a drawer close to the stove and discovered that it wasn't empty.

"Look, Paula." She turned, holding up a floral apron and an old, wooden box. She shook out the apron, which was covered in a pattern of red roses and trimmed with lace, like something from the '40s, when women cooked all afternoon and then served their men cocktails before dinner. She tied it around her waist and gave a twirl. "What do you think?"

"You look like Betty Crocker. Hey, are those old recipes?" Paula reached for the box. It was full of recipe cards. The ink was faded, but the handwriting on the cards was still clear. She flipped through them, calling out names: Mincemeat Nut Rolls, Almond Crescent Cookies, Lemon Flummery, Kentucky Chess Pie.

Shelly was disappointed; she was hoping for Ginger-Glazed Pork Chops or Grandma Bette's Green Bean Almondine, but they were all desserts. "Too bad."

"Why's that? These sound fun." She flipped through a few more. "You could bake something for the party."

"I don't have a sweet tooth."

Paula arched her eyebrow. "I don't believe that. What happened, did your mom spank you with the kitchen spoons for swiping cookies when you were a kid?"

Shelly turned away to put the glasses in a cupboard. "Um, no. I just have to watch what I eat, you know?"

"Why, you're such a gorgeous young thing." Paula put her arms around Shelly's waist and bent to kiss her behind the ear. Shelly was petite and pear-shaped, both things she'd always hated. She wanted to be tall and slender, like Paula.

"Hey, you two, cut that out." Karen, Paula's girlfriend, came in with another box.

"Okay, okay. I was just reassuring our sweet Shelly how

much I like her shape." Paula patted Shelly on the ass, which made her blush. They'd been friends for a long time, but never lovers.

"I agree, but she has to find her own girl. You're with me." Karen kissed both of them and left to get another box.

"Thanks for helping me move," Shelly said, to try and change the subject.

"Of course. You found such a cute place. But you really should bake something for the housewarming party. And wear the apron. It's really sexy."

Two weeks later, Shelly had finally unpacked enough boxes to have the housewarming party. She invited Paula and Karen, plus three other girlfriends, to come celebrate. Paula offered to bring a lasagna, and she demanded Shelly bake something from the recipe box. Shelly grudgingly agreed. She decided she could make something, but she didn't have to eat any of it.

There was a recipe for blondies that looked simple: melted butter, brown sugar, an egg, flour, baking powder, salt and vanilla. She had an old pan that seemed about the right size. As she stirred the ingredients in a bowl she usually used for salads, she found herself humming. The kitchen smelled wonderful when the blondies were baking. She lay down to catch a quick nap before everyone came. The kitchen timer would wake her up in time.

Shelly's dream was full of swirling figures, dancing around the bed. She tried to make out who was there, but everything was foggy. One pale figure came closer and leaned over her. Warm lips met hers and Shelly felt the press of a tongue, which explored her mouth and teased her own tongue into joining the game. Cool fingers stroked her skin, trailing from her shoulder to her hip. She arched up toward the mouth but the figure was

gone. She struggled up from the twisted sheets when she realized the buzzer was going off. She rushed into the kitchen and
pulled the blondies out of the oven. They were a lovely golden-
brown. She touched her lips, remembering the heated kiss.

Paula and Karen came at dusk with the lasagna. While
Shelly was putting it in the oven to stay warm, the doorbell rang
again. Karen ushered in the rest of the guests: Kit and Frances
brought flowers and Angela carried a bottle of cold champagne
as a housewarming gift. Shelly opened it and they all sipped
champagne as she showed them around.

Over dinner, they talked about living in old houses. Kit
wondered if the house was haunted.

"I haven't heard any ghosts yet," Shelly said, laughing, "but
I did have a weird dream this afternoon. I took a nap while the
blondies were baking, and I dreamed that my room was full of
people dancing."

"They started the party without us." Karen pouted. Paula,
however, had heard the word baking and was all over it. "What
were you baking?"

"Oh, no, the party is right here." Shelly stalled as she collected
the dinner plates. "It was nothing. Just a dream." She returned
from the kitchen with a covered plate, set it down in the middle
of the table and whipped off the towel. "Voila!" Underneath sat
a pile of the blondies.

Karen reached for one and took a bite. "These are good,
Shell, where did you buy them?"

"I didn't buy them. I'll have you know, I made them myself."

"You didn't." Kit was surprised, but Paula smiled.

Everyone knew how badly Shelly cooked. "She found some
recipes when she moved in and I made a few demands," Paula
said. She went into the kitchen and returned holding the box
and the apron. "Don't forget to show them the apron."

"Oh, yeah, give us a spin," "Yeah, put it on," the other women urged her, in a rising chorus of voices.

Shelly felt silly wearing the apron, but she put it on and twirled around once, arms over her head like a ballerina. Everyone laughed and no one noticed that she wasn't eating any of the blondies.

"Well, I hope you make more demands. These are good." Angela took another blondie and passed around the wine.

"Maybe we should pick something for her to make next weekend," Karen suggested.

"We can make it a regular event," Kit added.

Paula passed the box around and they pulled out recipes, exclaiming over ones they knew or things they'd never heard of.

"Here's something called Cherry Claffouti. How about that?" Paula waved a card at the group.

"What about this one?" Kit suggested. "Panaforte Siena. Don't know what it is, but it has chocolate in it."

"Wait, guys. Be reasonable. Pick something simple. You know I'm terrible in the kitchen."

"I bet you're not as bad as we'd like," Frances said, and winked at her, making Shelly blush.

"Okay, here's a cookie recipe that should be right up your alley. Nancy's Chocolate Dainties." Paula handed the card to Shelly with an air of finality.

The ingredients were simple enough and they sounded good. "All right, I'll make them, but you all have to come and eat them. And bring more wine." Shelly raised her empty glass in Angela's direction and she filled it for her.

After they'd finished the wine and the rest of the blondies. Paula helped Shelly with the dishes.

"The blondies were a hit, sexy girl." Paula winked at Shelly as she filled the sink with hot water.

"Beginner's luck."

"Well, we'll see about that next weekend."

They finished the dishes and everyone left. Shelly caught sight of herself in the mirror as she undressed for bed. Her hips seemed wider than before, even though she hadn't eaten any dessert. Her mother had always told her that desserts went straight to the hips and Shelly believed it. Despite what Paula had said, she didn't think she looked sexy at all.

Shelly worked hard and dieted all week, in anticipation of more baking. She checked out the recipe and realized there was more to making Nancy's Chocolate Dainties than she'd thought. She had to buy some ingredients, as well as a new pan to bake the cookies on, and the dough had to be made the night before, so it could be chilled. Thursday night, after work, she got started. The recipe instructed her to beat the softened butter with the sugar until it looked fluffy and then mix in all the other ingredients. She patted the dough into a disk and wrapped it in plastic wrap to put in the fridge, but she couldn't resist breaking off a piece of the raw dough to eat. She felt very naughty eating it. The dough was a rich, dark chocolate, the color of wet dirt, and it tasted spicy and mysterious.

The smell of cinnamon lingered when she finally went to sleep. She woke in the middle of the night for no reason and reached out for her alarm clock: 3:12 a.m. It was warm in the room, so she pulled off her nightshirt and slid over to the cooler side of the bed. Just as she was falling into a dream, she felt warm lips on her neck. She stretched and brushed back her hair so that her dream visitor could kiss further. The lips continued to kiss from under her ear to the base of her throat. Once again, cool fingers brushed her shoulder, and this time, they trailed down between her breasts, nails tickling the skin under each breast as they passed. Her nipples tightened and she arched her back, wishing for them to be sucked.

Shelly felt a hot mouth suck one nipple hard against teeth.
She reached out and felt the soft skin of her dream lover. Teeth
nipped at her breast, sending a curl of heat straight to her pussy.
She spread her legs and moaned, *Yes*. She felt skin sliding against
skin, breasts against breasts, and she wanted to take them in
her hands, cup them and taste them. Her half-formed desires
dissolved as fingers found their way between her legs and began
drawing secret designs on the folds of her flesh.

Cool arms wrapped around her hips and long hair spilled
across her thighs. Shelly lifted her body to the dream lover's
mouth, wanting more pressure, more friction. The smell of
cinnamon filled her head as her lover's tongue flicked against
her clit. Two fingers and then three began to stroke into her
pussy and Shelly gasped for air. She could feel her orgasm
building, like a kettle about to whistle as it boils. She tightened
her thighs against her lover's body and thrashed as she came.
She moaned and bit her lip, shuddering as the dream lover's
tongue thrummed across her clit. The orgasm continued rolling
through her. "No, no, please." Her cries cut through the heat
of the dream and Shelly woke, trembling, tangled in the sheets.
She reached a hand between her legs and felt the power of her
dream in her wetness and still throbbing clit. She lay back. Who
was this woman? A ghost? The dream lover did not return and
Shelly finally fell into a deep sleep until the alarm woke her.

After work, she cut the chilled cookies into rounds and laid
them on the parchment-covered pan. As they baked, the scent
of cinnamon rose in the air and she remembered the dream. A
shiver ran down her neck as the smell of cookies combined with
the scent of her arousal. Maybe learning to bake was a good
idea after all.

That night, the friends convened for dinner. Kit and Frances brought Chinese takeout and they all drank the German beer Karen brought. Everyone was waiting for the cookies, to see how they had turned out, but Shelly wouldn't let them have one until after dinner. The cookies were a big hit. Karen suggested that they make this a regular weekly event; they searched through the recipes and found several more for Shelly to attempt. Shelly wanted to tell Paula about the dreams, how the ghostly lover seemed to come when she baked, but it sounded just a little too crazy.

She fell asleep reading, with the light on. This time, the dream was different. Shelly was sitting at the kitchen table, eating cookies. A beautiful woman walked into the room. She was naked except for a short, floral apron, the one Shelly had found in the drawer. Although she was taller than Shelly, she was just as round and curvy. Her full breasts swayed as she moved and Shelly couldn't stop looking at the plump red nipples that crowned them.

"Would you like a cookie?" Shelly offered her the plate. The naked woman said nothing, just sat across from Shelly and helped herself to the stack of Chocolate Dainties. Shelly watched her eat one after the other; the plate remained full, and yet the woman ate and ate. Finally, she stopped eating and licked her lips. Shelly couldn't take her eyes off the woman's dark pink tongue as it sought the crumbs still clinging to her mouth.

The woman stood and walked around to Shelly's chair; she lifted Shelly's hair and kissed her behind the right ear. "I love the way you bake," she whispered. She pulled Shelly to her feet and led her to the bedroom, letting the apron fall in the kitchen doorway. They fell onto the bed, tongues and limbs tangled together, tasting of cinnamon.

Shelly cupped her dream lover's breasts and bent to take those succulent nipples in her mouth. They tasted of licorice.

Her skin was as soft as butter. The woman rolled them over and straddled her hips, grinding her mound against Shelly's. She leaned down and kissed Shelly, her tongue darting into the dreaming woman's mouth. Their breasts pressed together and Shelly could feel her own nipples stiffen. She wiggled her hips, caught in the other's strong embrace.

As Shelly stroked her lover's breasts, they became mounds of butter: cool and moldable under her fingers. Her lover's pussy became a hill of crystal sugar, merging with the butter to form a delicious dough. Sweet drips of vanilla came from her pussy, flavoring the dough and creating a heady perfume in the room. Her lover traced Shelly's lips and when she opened to suck them, her mouth was filled with sweetness. She nibbled at almond-paste fingers, tasting strawberries and cream, salted caramel, dense roasted nuts. Every inch of Shelly's skin was alive with the touch of silky flour, gritty sugar, melting butter. She felt languid and lovely, never once thinking of what her mother would say about her hips. She trembled under her dream lover's caresses, as they found her clit and circled it. The sweetness made her head spin and her pussy ache. She clenched her muscles around phantom fingers, drawing them farther and farther into herself. She cried out as her orgasm rushed through her. Shelly felt a warm curtain of melted chocolate fall over them, enrobing their bodies in a delicious glaze. Her lover settled against her, skin on skin, the smell of burnt sugar in the air, and Shelly slept.

In the morning, Shelly woke at dawn, feeling sticky and sore. Her room smelled like a bakery and her sheets were gritty. Smiling, she walked to the kitchen, stepping over the apron, and reached for the box of recipes.

THE GIRL ON THE EGYPTIAN ESCALATOR

NJ Streitberger

S pencer could hear her from the top of the escalator. Having spent a frustrating hour trawling the china and glass department for a glass bowl to replace the one that had recently been sent to punchbowl heaven, he was irritated, tired and somewhat in need of a drink.

It was his own fault. Sale season was rarely conducive to effective decision-making and he regretted entering the building almost as much as smashing Laura's bowl.

He had encountered Laura at a charity ball held at the Natural History Museum a year earlier. She had been accompanied by an American hedge-fund manager whose swarthy appearance and pit-bull aggression had seemed entirely out of keeping with the pale, willowy blonde draped languidly on his arm. Spencer had been in a party of colleagues from the bank who were some of the charity's biggest patrons and had found himself sitting next to her during the lavish dinner. Her companion, whom Spencer had immediately dubbed "the Neanderthal," had eaten little, perspired a lot and absented himself from the table more times than was strictly necessary, leaving Laura alone with a wobbly, apologetic smile and an unspoken but evident entreaty to be rescued.

Spencer had done the honorable thing and seduced her. When she had taken him home to meet Mummy and Daddy he detected less a sense of approval than relief at the fact that he was Anglo-Saxon, British born and had decent prospects in a more respectable branch of the much-maligned world of high finance.

Consequently, he had felt himself evolving into the kind of man that his relentlessly middle-class mother had always wondered why he couldn't be more like. He had even adopted their way of referring to their local store as the "corner shop" run by that "loathsome little rug merchant."

Now this. A frustrating, panic-induced trip to the "rug-merchant's corner shop." He had just managed to secure a place on the top step, having narrowly escaped castration on one of the poles placed strategically for that very purpose at the head of each escalator, after a double-wide American woman had tailgated him like a Mack truck, when *her* voice scoured his ears.

"What are you thinking of? You are a complete loser! I don't know why I bother. You're a total waste of space. How can you be so fucking stupid all the time?"

Intrigued in spite of himself, he stared down at the ascending escalator, trying to find the creature responsible and the poor sap to whom the torrent of abuse was directed. Finally, after peering past swarthy men in designer stubble and bottle-blonde broomsticks, he saw her.

Uh-oh.

She was standing on the step above her victim, with her back toward him. He could see the wild, raven hair, tossing around as she spewed her verbal venom without surcease, her shoulder blades tensing and shifting beneath her skintight jacket like a wild animal struggling to escape a net. He watched as her hands gesticulated wildly, taking in the crowded escalator like the audience in a packed theater. Beneath her, the poor sap simply stood, looking like a little boy being given a terrible telling-off by his headmistress.

With a half smile of humiliation playing around his lips, the object of her contempt simply stood looking up at her rapt in a combination of self-loathing, wry amusement and sheer admiration. He was easily as tall as her, athletically slim with dark curly hair and a sharp nose. A handsome boy, he thought. Thoroughly undeserving of this blatantly public act of humiliation.

As the two of them approached with agonizing slowness, she suddenly turned around and their gazes met and locked. Her eyes flashed with an almost feral light, her mouth was curved in a way that was half sneer, half snarl. The poor fellow might have been wearing the trousers, but there was no doubt about who was the alpha creature in this relationship.

Spencer couldn't tear his eyes away. She saw him and stared straight through him, challenging him to say something. He clammed up, unable even to open his mouth. As they passed each other on the escalator, he descending, she ascending, he had the ridiculous compulsion to leap across the barrier between them and grab her, clutch her wild and vibrating body against his and take her right there, right then, on the bloody escalator.

Christ. He hadn't had that kind of jolt for years.

She continued to stare at him, their heads twisting as they passed, as if their eyes were linked by an invisible thread. His insides felt funny, as though someone was messing about in his bowels. Eventually, she gave a kind of snort and a sneer and turned her face back toward her victim. He seemed smaller, shrunken in the process, as if some vampire had sucked the life essence out of him, leaving him a husk hanging on to the handrail of the escalator. He was, he thought, ready for the sarcophagus, doubtless inspired by the elaborate Egyptian fakery of the walls and the decorative plasterwork surrounding the escalator. He was mummified, the living dead.

Poor sod.

Spencer reached the bottom of the escalator and tried to look back up but was prevented from standing still by the avalanche of bodies coming after him; he caught a glimpse of her swaying raven hair as she stepped off the end of the moving staircase. Oddly, he could not see the about-to-be ex-boyfriend at all. He seemed to have disappeared. All this was academic, however, as he was immediately caught in the surging crowd and was swept out toward the front doors of the store and soon found himself standing in the street.

He wandered along Knightsbridge in a kind of dream state for a while, idly staring into shop windows not because he wanted to but because it was expected of him. It was a kind of Pavlovian reaction. Look. Want. Acquire.

If only he hadn't looked.

He tried to distract himself by considering the need for a pair of Church's half-brogues, reduced to the not-unreasonable sum of £160. He knew he already owned a pair of brogues but a chap can never have enough shoes. He passed on, wandering into Uniqlo and idly sorting through the skinny-fit jeans that were reduced by 30 percent with an extra 10 percent discount at the till if bought today. He needed another pair of jeans like a hole in the head.

He knew what he was doing. Displacement activity, it was called. He went back into Knightsbridge and tried to urge his feet toward the Victoria & Albert Museum. Culture would cure his ills!

He was just about to cross the road when he stopped dead in his tracks, causing a man with a mobile phone clamped fiercely to his ear to bump into him and swear, before sidestepping him with a vicious glance and an undercover oath.

Without thinking about it, Spencer turned back and started walking toward the store he had just left.

Once he had entered, he headed straight for the Egyptian escalator, pushing and shoving his way through the crowds to get on and studying every face and figure as he ascended. He went right to the top of the store and raced through each department, trying to retrace his steps and at the same time attempting to imagine which department she was likely to have been headed for. He searched in vain and eventually wound up back on the escalator, descending disconsolately to the ground floor, taking one last desultory look at the people who passed him, ignoring their hostile glares.

As he stepped off at the bottom he saw her standing by the door, looking at him.

"Having fun?" she said, with a Vivien Leigh–like arch of an eyebrow.

"I thought..." he began, changing tack halfway through. "Where's your friend?"

"He's history," she said, leading the way out of the store.

Shirt buttons popped and flew across the room and expensive La Perla silk tore as they attacked each other in her Flood Street flat. There was no time to think, no time to consider the folly of their union. It was crazed, feral, sweaty, slippery-slidey, crawling-all-over-each-other sex. He drank in her odors, nuzzling her nipples into hardness and sucking on the miniature pink volcanoes. He delighted in her unshaven armpits, slick with musky sweat, and felt her hand beneath his balls, pulling him inside her. In their frenzy they fell off the bed, still engaged in loin-to-loin combat, and rolled across the floor until he had her pinned against the wall, side by side as he rammed so hard into her it was though he wanted to push her through the wall into the next room, or the next dimension. She had one hand on his shoulder, digging her nails into his flesh for purchase and the other on his buttock, pumping him into her. She bit his chin as she climaxed, drawing blood, and he howled as he reached his own orgasm.

After some moments of breathlessness, they subsided and he collapsed onto his back, flopping out of her. She stood and stepped over him, walking toward the kitchen. In a blur he watched the sway of her sweat-slicked bottom, admiring the shameless manner of her stride, which revealed the soaked tuft of dark fur between her thighs and the way she stretched her arms upward to ease the muscles.

Bloody Hell, he thought. *What have I got myself into here?*

He heard a bang and sat up, vaguely nervous. She came back into the room, holding a bottle of champagne. She swigged straight from the bottle and scattered some of it over his cooling body before handing him the bottle. He drank, coughed and drank again.

"I love the Sales," she said. "You never know what you're going to find."

It couldn't last, of course. Not at that level of intensity. He did his best and, to be sure, she inspired him to extraordinary feats of stamina that surprised him. She was nothing like Laura, whose enthusiasm in bed was tempered with a well-bred polite-ness that he now realized was a terrible turn-off. Laura always came with a delicate "Oh-Oh-Oh!" and then immediately took a shower and brewed a cup of Lapsang.

Sekhmet, on the other hand, was an animal. She just threw on her clothes and took him out to San Lorenzo still stinking of sex, often rubbing her hand over his crotch underneath the table as he tried to eat his asparagus risotto without groaning.

"Where did you get a name like that, anyway?" he asked her, when he could breathe again after a particularly savage workout.

"I was named after an Egyptian goddess," she said.

"That's funny," he said. "You don't look Egyptian."

She struck him playfully, leaving talon-marks on his cheek.

"My friends call me Seksie," she said, licking blood from his lacerated skin.

"I can't begin to imagine why," he whimpered as she wrapped her fingers around his aching cock.

It didn't take long for Laura to realize there was something amiss. Exhausted by Sekhmet's insatiable appetites, he was unable to fulfill Laura's relatively modest requirements. It was when she noticed a particularly musky smell on his shirt that she twigged. There were tears, recriminations and the *Summoning of the Parents*. As far as they were concerned, he was toast. He moved out of the flat they had bought together in Queensgate Place and into a rented studio in Earl's Court, which in spite of their proximity was a bit like moving from Maidenhead to Mars.

In his little kitchenette, Spencer poured a glass of shiraz and wondered where his life was going. Clearly, he was in the throes of sexual obsession and, although he felt regret at the loss of Laura and all that she represented—wealth, respectability, comfort—he was inclined to believe that he had made,

albeit by default, the correct decision. Marriage to Laura would
have evolved too quickly into a plateau hemmed in by a narrow
circle of friends whose social circumstances kept them circling
the same limited pool of interests. Charity balls, dinner parties,
property portfolios, art to be collected rather than admired and
explored. No, it was not for him. Boredom would have set in.
It would have been far too restricting. All things considered, he
was better off without her. Even so, he wondered just how long
he would be able to keep up with his new companion.

He started to fade at work, exhausted to the point that his
concentration ebbed. As the markets collapsed, he lost the edge
he needed now more than ever to shift and sell, buy and jettison.
The computer screens blurred, his mind slowed down, clotted
with images of Sekhmet. Physically, he was a ruin. His body
was one big bruise.

He was summoned into Sir Trevor's office.

"What the devil's going on, Spencer? Your figures are atro-
cious. We're all in the same boat here and we cannot afford this
kind of slippage. Are you on drugs?"

"God, no. No, sir…" he stammered. "I, just, er, I'm a bit
tired that's all."

"Tired? Tired!" exploded Sir Trevor. "You can't afford to
be tired. Nobody can these days. This is your one and only
warning. Shape up or ship out."

He went back to his station, depressed and totally demoti-
vated.

"You wimp," she said, when he unwisely told her of his troubles
at work. "Why didn't you tell him where to get off?"

"Because I'll never get another position like this. The market
is already overcrowded. And there are plenty of younger chaps

out there just itching to step into my shoes. There's a recession on, you know. In case you hadn't noticed."

Clearly, she hadn't. Whatever it was that she did, which remained a mystery to him, Sekhmet was evidently well heeled. Her flat in Chelsea was spectacular, filled with expensive objets d'art of museum quality, however she acquired them. Yet she treated everything around her with a cavalier disregard for its value. In the throes of passion, they had smashed at least two Chinese vases from the Tang Dynasty and toppled a Roman sculpture, chipping off an ear—events which would have caused apoplexy in any curator. Sekhmet simply brushed the pieces into a black plastic bag and dumped them in the dustbin.

"What do you, er, do?" he asked Sekhmet as she untangled herself from the sheets and stood up.

"I'm a consultant," she said over her shoulder and went into the kitchen to locate a bottle of champagne.

"Who are your, uh, consultees?" he asked, attempting to rise from the wrecked bed.

"Oh, you know. The British Museum. The Egyptian Museum in Cairo. Places like that."

"I see." He didn't.

"Anyway, why do you want to know?"

"No reason. It's just…"

"Where do you think you're going?" she asked, pushing him back down onto the bed. "We've only just started."

Oh, Christ, he thought.

"I hope you're thirsty," she said, looking down at him, swinging the freshly popped bottle of bubbly from one hand like a club.

"Yes," he said. "Parched, actually."

"Good. Stay there and don't move."

She lay on her back beside him, raised her hips and opened her legs. While he watched, fascinated, she inserted the neck of the bottle between the ever-hungry lips of her cunt and tilted it upward, emptying the contents inside her.

Oh, my god, he thought, suspecting what was to follow.

She tossed the empty bottle aside, knocking an ancient Greek amphora off a plinth onto the floor, where it broke into thirteen pieces.

Pinning his shoulders to the bed with her strong hands, she sat astride him, sliding her wet cunt up his chest until she was sitting astride his face. Positioning herself over his lips, she relaxed her vaginal muscles and pissed the newly aromatized champagne into his open mouth. He drank and gagged, choked and spluttered as the foaming liquid sluiced down his throat and entered his nose, virtually drowning him in a stream of vintage Bollinger and *Eau de Vulva.*

As it ended and he started to get his breath back, she lowered herself onto his face and began rubbing herself back and forth over his lips and nose, smothering him in her musky, salty, champagney cunt.

"Stick out your tongue," she commanded. "Make it stiff."

She rubbed faster, sliming his face with a combination of juices and secretions, locating his nose with her engorged clitoris.

As she moved faster and faster, her orgasm rising from her center of operations, Spencer felt that his features were being rubbed away and that he would end up a faceless zombie doomed to roam the city streets after dark. The Erased Man.

She roared as she came, clawing the wall in her ecstasy.

A little while afterward, she flicked his flaccid cock with a contemptuous fingernail.

"Well, lover. What shall we do now?" she asked, with a cruel curve of her mouth.

Too drunk to fuck and too fucked to drink, he could do nothing but groan in reply.

The following morning, having called in sick, he looked up the number of the British Museum and dialed. Three tablets of Berocca fizzed noisily in a glass on his faux-granite kitchen counter.

"British Museum."

"Hello. Can you put me through to the Egyptology Department?"

"Certainly, sir. Hold for one moment, please."

Three seconds passed.

"Egyptology."

"Oh, yes. Hello. I am trying to trace one of your consultants. I am doing some research and someone gave me her name as a possibly useful contact."

"I see. What is the name?"

"Sekhmet."

"Sekhmet what?"

"I'm sorry, I don't know."

"Is this some sort of joke?"

"Oh no, not at all. But I assume there can't be many people with that name working there."

"I can assure you, sir, that there is no one of that name working here or associated with the museum. Not alive, at any rate."

Spencer's scalp tingled.

"What do you mean?"

"Sekhmet is the name of an ancient Egyptian deity. There are several extant images of her in existence. It is highly unlikely that anyone would name their daughter after her."

"Why would that be?"

"Because she is considered the most formidable and destructive of the Egyptian gods. She is usually depicted with the head of a lion. In the Ancient Egyptian world her name is synonymous with overwhelming female power and bloodshed. She is also known as the Mistress of Dread or the Lady of Slaughter."

"Oh, er, I..."

"Now, if you've quite finished wasting my time, I have better things to do. Good-bye, sir."

The line went dead. Spencer put the receiver back very, very gently.

The crunch came when he failed to perform one Saturday afternoon, after she grabbed him on the sofa where he had been dozing in front of a particularly important match in the Six Nations Championship.

She stood over him, having pulled on her jeans without bothering with underwear, and sneered down at him.

"Time to go," she said. "The Sales are on."

"Oh, no," he groaned. "There are loads of sales. Why now?"

"There is only *one*," she said.

And so he found himself standing on the Egyptian escalator as she spat her venom at him. Too tired to respond in kind, diminished and defeated, he suffered the agonies of public humiliation in a kind of bewildered daze, like a naughty little boy or a dog who had peed on the carpet.

"You're useless!" she screamed, glaring down at him from the step above. "Call yourself a man? You're so fucking wet you should be going out with a sponge, not a real woman. You're nothing but a loser. Go back to Mummy, loser!"

Although he was dimly aware of people staring at him he

just stood and took it, a half smile on his lips.

"Look at me when I'm talking to you! See? You can't even look me in the eyes. Where is your spunk? I don't know what I ever saw in you."

He was about to say something when she turned and stared across at the descending escalator. A young blond man with a rugged, weather-beaten face and an athletic figure was staring at them with amusement. He looked pityingly at Spencer who could do nothing but smile stupidly back and watch as the guy turned his attention to Sekhmet. Spencer recognized the look— the blond guy was experiencing the same impact that had struck him a few months earlier. *Don't,* he thought. *Don't look. And whatever you do, don't turn back. You'll be sorry.*

But it was too late. The guy was hooked.

Spencer was so weak he couldn't summon the energy to challenge her, to resist the inevitable. Trailing behind her he could feel himself growing smaller. It was an illusion, of course, a manifestation of his psychological diminution.

All the same, when the escalator reached the top and Sekhmet walked off, she heard a woman who was standing two steps behind her comment in a conspicuously loud voice: "God, this place is filthy. Look at that pile of dust. You'd think that loathsome little rug merchant could afford to employ decent cleaning staff."

Not that it mattered. Spencer was nowhere to be seen. And by the time the escalator had completed its circuit, the pile of dust was gone for good.

THE SORCERER'S CATCH

Angela Caperton

Now I have you," the young man in the black robe said.

He spoke the truth. Anastasia was pinned within the magic circle drawn in red paint around the man's bed, trapped as securely as the least devil in the hands of Faust himself.

The magician—the first conjurer she had met in the twenty-first century—had drawn his circle tightly enough that Ana could not move off the bed even a single step, so she knelt there on red silk sheets, trying to look demure. She had approached his bed gowned in smoke and when he had sprung his trap, bringing her out of dreams and into his world, the smoke solidified into black lace, draping her ivory skin like alluring spiderwebs that left her all but naked before his direct gaze.

She covered her breasts, gratified by the disappointment in his eyes. He was very young, no more than twenty-five years old. Was he powerful in his magic or just lucky?

"What shall I call you?" she asked him, trying not to sound surly.

"Adam." She had hoped he would be stupid enough to tell her his real name, but she knew at once that he had given a false one.

"What do you want of me, Adam?" The name would suffice for now. It said something about him that he chose *that* name. "What must I do to be free again?"

"First, Anastasia, you will teach me," he said. From within his robe, he produced four golden chains, delicate things, like jewelry, but she sensed the inscriptions on the links: binding runes that would cage her.

He looped her wrists and ankles, pulled tight and spread her faceup on the crimson sheets. He touched her with strong, firm hands; spoke words of protection as he worked, careful, as though fearful of releasing some demon inside her.

No, she conceded as he finished forcing her legs well apart, he was not stupid.

When Adam finished his work, he had bound her to the four posts of the bed and she lay helpless before him. The situation was not unpleasant, even though she faced the direst sort of danger.

"Teach you what?" she asked, tugging the unyielding chains, testing them.

He watched for a moment then reached down to part her robe of webs, baring her breasts and belly and the little wisp of lacy shadow that covered her pussy.

"Carnal knowledge," he replied formally. "Teach me all things, both lawful and forbidden."

He had called her by her favorite name, Anastasia, a name she had taken from the dream of a Bolshevik soldier long ago. The man had guarded the Romanoff family in Ipatiev's house and, days later, after the soldier had helped to kill the girl, he dreamed

about her. His guilt and obsession had drawn the attention of
a bored succubus. It had heralded a new beginning for Ana,
awakened her to the dawning century and the grand dreams of
men and women with plans to remake the world.

When the whims of dreamers demanded another name, she
would take one, to seduce and entice, but Anastasia had become
the name she called herself for almost a hundred years.

And now this young wizard, this barely grown man, had
summoned her by her name, in the voice of rituals unspoken in
three generations, drawn her with the rich lure of her own curiosity. She had descended into his dream and his magic circle had
closed like a foothold trap. Now she lay bound to his bed.

"Wait," she breathed, as he reached for the wisp of her
panties.

He regarded her for a moment then proceeded with his
intention. His fingers burned like brands and her garment disin-
tegrated, fragile as smoke. Ana had the sudden fear that her
flesh might prove as delicate. Her gasp barely seemed real as it
passed her lips.

Adam liked that, a tight smile betraying his delight. Then
he turned his gaze directly into her eyes. "I cannot wait." He
wet his fingers and rubbed the bud of her clit. He wasn't bad
looking at all, hollow cheeks and serious, beautiful eyes, with
strong, smooth hands. Her pussy slicked at his touch, her nature
dependable even in dire circumstance. He dropped his robe, an
acolyte approaching the altar, prayed in Sumerian, then probed
the wet line of her pussy end to end, opening her.

She rose in the chains, enough to see his cock just as he put
it in her, a respectable appendage, wonderfully hard and ready.
Her vision clouded with the bliss of penetration. This was better
than a dream. His chains held her while he fucked her with
hard, expert thrusts, his hands raising her butt and stroking

her anus and crack. She bucked against him as best she could, but there was little question of cooperation. He fucked her with purpose and she, who had once toppled an empire by touching the dreams of a queen, was helpless to do much but take it, and to come almost at once, then again and again, before Adam finally erupted inside her, his precious seed hot and alive.

He stroked her hips, his touch efficient but almost tender as he withdrew stickily.

"Now maybe we can talk a little, eh?" she asked him with a little laugh and a punctuating tinkle of chains.

He smiled—full of afterglow, she imagined, and replied, "The old books say I should only ask you questions and tell you nothing."

"That's a start. Can you unbind me?"

"And if I do?" he asked, smirking as he donned his robe again. She hated to see him cover up. She would have to rely on more subtle visual clues to know when she had aroused him again and, well, he had a nice-looking cock, even spent. She settled on his beautiful eyes for an alternate indicator of his passion. Analytical and inquisitive eyes, but she had seen real fire there too, and she knew she could kindle it again.

"So, what do you want to know?" She tried to sit up but her wrist chains held her. He worked on the headboard a moment and lengthened the span of her bonds. Still cuffed, she had more room to move. She sat upright and he settled at the foot, just out of her reach, his silk-robed thigh a quarter inch from her bare calf.

"How old are you?"

"A meaningless question, Adam. I have always been."

"What happens to men and women when we die?"

"I don't know."

He frowned, but nodded, accepting her ignorance. She didn't

care if he believed her. Her answer was truthful.

"Do you remember a man named Herbert Stanley?"

She shook her head and smiled. "Often I know only the names mortals wear in dreams. I might remember him if I saw his picture."

"It doesn't matter. Mr. Stanley gave me the crucial information to find you, Anastasia. It was in his records that I first read your name."

"I don't understand." She had certainly given her name to hundreds of souls within dreams, but it had never occurred to her that they might remember or share the knowledge once they woke.

"I'm a psychologist, Ana. Do you know what that is?"

"Of course: a physician of the mind."

"My family also has a tradition of magick—we have been summoning imps and spirits for almost two hundred years. I've been learning that craft too. You might be surprised at how many people share my twin professions."

"Clearly you have surpassed your ancestors," she purred with a touch of playfulness. "They *might* be proud." She smiled as she said it, and arched her back. In dreams she would have shaped herself to his desires, but in the flesh, she had to rely on simpler bait. Her nipples drew his gaze.

He laughed. "Do you want something to cover you?"

"By the nightmare, no! Why would I want that?" She smiled at him, spirits of purest mischief playing in her mind. "Tell me about this man," she said. "This Mr. Stanley."

"There's not much to tell. He was a policeman in…Boston, if I remember right. His case study was part of my research in my first year of postgraduate study. He was classified as schizophrenic, but the details of his dreams were especially well documented. You made quite an impression on him. One thing led to another. Do you know that tens of thousands of case studies are available now in digital files? Searching them isn't hard. You've left quite a trail in the treatment records of doctors all over the world."

"If any of these patients said I caused them harm, they are lying."

Adam stroked her calf, the top of her foot, and brushed the sole, tickling delightfully. "We do not always know the harm we cause, Anastasia."

"I gave them dreams."

"Yes, and then you took them away. The more I read, the more convinced I became that you were probably the same... figment...in patient cases that went all the way back to the early alienists. Before that, I found your traces in madhouse diaries and church records. I know a lot about you, Anastasia."

She stretched her ankle chain to its limit and pinched the muscle of his robed thigh with her toes. "You don't know anything about me."

He jumped and laughed. "I didn't expect you to be like this," he said. "You're easy to talk to."

"I am so much more than that."

The fire had returned to his eyes and he tossed his robe aside, already impressively hard. He left her wrists enough play to allow her to hold him while he sat astride the bed, her butt cradled in his lap as he pulled her onto his erection. *Rituals of domination,* she mused, *wand and chalice.* She hummed. The wand fit the chalice perfectly, thank you very much.

He fucked her the second time with more concentration, attentive to her every movement but focused on his own pleasure and on making her the slave of his strength. Her legs ached with wanting to wrap him, but the chains held her back, entirely at his mercy. Since he'd already come once, she judged that his endurance would be improved. He did not disappoint her. Merciless, he ignored her sweat and the little cries that escaped her control and fucked her with long, deep strokes; a flesh pistoning machine better than any dream lover, insatiable and inexhaustible; until an overwhelming, hot wave of orgasm rose from her cunt through her belly, along the arch of her spine, all the way to the bindings on her wrists and ankles.

Her mind vanished, blown to pieces, to starlight and darkest delight, and still he did not come.

"Adam," she cried. "Stop, I can't..." but another explosion took her, no slow building this time, but sudden, as surprising as thunder. Her substance wavered, her flesh thrilling, burning with pleasure. She became the moment of her ecstasy even as he erupted within her.

Drenched, sagging against him, his cock still in her, she whispered, "Incubus."

"What?" He pulled back and his spent prick jumped against her clit.

"Mmm," she whispered, grinding. "You should have been one."

He gripped her hips and she moved against him, trying to tempt his cock back to life, unwilling to let go, wanting him to fuck her one more time. After that, she would have to find a way to escape, even if she had to strangle him with the loosened chain.

"I am going to keep you," he promised, "until I have bound you to my will as you are bound to this bed. Every night for seven nights, I will make you scream. Then you must stay with me forever."

She recognized the rite, though she had not heard of it being performed since 1881 in Paris. Seven nights of relentless fucking, tender and savage passion. Sweat, tongues and finger play, sodomy and painful pleasure. Dusk till dawn. If he made her come each night, she would be bound to his will for the length of his mortal life. Anna had always thought the stories were fables.

"You don't need to do this," she told him. "I will serve you now."

Miracle! He had grown half hard inside her again. She fought the cuff on her right hand. She ached to touch him. He ran his thumb over her swollen clit, smearing their combined juices, wringing new cries from her lips at the fresh assault on flesh already pushed past its limit.

"No. The ritual must be run."

She remembered the best dreams she had made in the minds of good men and women, entire lifetimes lived in the hours between sleep and dawn. How many times had she become lost? How many times had she fallen in love? A hundred? A thousand? Those nights she spun the dream so true, she lived the years with her sleeping lover, lost herself in her own wish, in tenderness and the slow burn of pleasure become true love.

This is his dream, she thought. *Surrender to it,* her soul commanded.

He withdrew the magical manifestation of his renewed cock and pulled her close, unbinding her wrists. He held them encircled in his fingers, kissed her palms. She allowed him to tie her again, hands together and stretched back over her head. Foolish man not to trust her. She had given up all thoughts of strangling him.

He loosed her ankles entirely, so she opened herself to accommodate him, knowing him now, how he felt and how he fit. This time he thrust deeper, all the way to her center, his rod divine, full of heat and spice and life. Free now, she scissored her legs around his waist and pushed against him, servant to his will, slave to the rhythm of his thrusts.

The bed fell away and she hung by her manacled wrists, his to claim, all the knowledge of the mind and world, his to master; the muse of his arts, desire and magic and the endless labyrinth of human feeling. They transcended each other's bodies and she bathed in his will and nurtured him, granting him confidence and compassion.

He loved her.

And she loved him.

They came together in a rush of light, the dream evaporating like foam on a beach, leaving warm sand and the slow rock of waves against their dreaming skin

She rose before dawn, left him asleep in the bed, the magic circle gone with the morning light, only a dream she had embraced for her pleasure and his growth. He was not yet a sorcerer, but he would be one, as great as any who had ever lived.

Anastasia would see to that herself, for at least six nights more.

THE CHAPEL

J. S. Wayne

Father William Frazier bolted the door of the chapel and turned away, walking quickly down the aisle toward the altar. Instead of proceeding up behind it, he folded gratefully into the front-row pew on the left side of the aisle and waited for the quiet echoes of his footsteps to fade to nothing.

The cathedral hummed with activity throughout the day, and as devoted as Bill was to his flock, he was usually glad to shut the doors for the night and savor the solemn, hushed peace of the chapel. He used the quiet time to commune with the Power he bowed to, and reflect upon the state of his own soul, resolving the conflicts that his parishioners embroiled him in and the myriad sins that weighed him down.

Tonight, the multitude of infractions seemed to weigh more heavily than usual, and the silence, rather than being a balm to his soul, settled over him like a shroud.

He'd buried his predecessor that very afternoon, which probably had much to do with the gloomy, almost morbid turn of his thoughts. Like most of the attendees at St. Katherine's, he had thought very highly of Father Michael Deidrich and his calm, quiet faith. To see such a man laid low had been a painful reminder that no matter how good a person might be, all returned to dust in the end. Worse, with Father Michael gone, it was now left to him, a priest just three years out of seminary, to carve his own niche as the spiritual voice of his flock.

He was very aware of every error he had made in the funerary rites, though none of the parishioners had seemed to notice. Bill had, and he hoped that the powers that keep track of such things had not seen fit to deny Michael his rightful place because of his apprentice's failures.

A tear welled up and dropped silently to the floor as Bill knelt on the prie-dieu in front of him. "Lord, grant him rest and a place among your saints," he prayed. "Let me be a fitting legacy and a worthy vessel for your command and his life's work."

From behind him came a tiny swishing sound of cloth in motion. With a quick swipe across his eyes, he turned and stood in one motion.

The woman who stood there, just on the razor's edge between the sallow illumination of the votives and the shadows beyond, was blindingly beautiful. Her lush frame was draped in a sheath of shimmering indigo. The planes of her face were sharp and soft all at once. Her sculpted eyebrows enticed the eye down her graceful nose to the delicate petals of her lips. Her eyes gleamed with liquid darkness, her neck was slender and graceful, and her deep blue dress hugged her generous curves in a way that was modest and sensual at the same time.

His pulse sped and his palms grew damp. The woman exuded sexual magnetism in a way that would require a much stronger man than Bill to ignore.

After a long silence, fraught with electricity, he finally cleared his throat and found his voice.

"I'm sorry. I didn't realize anyone was still here."

Her lips turned up in a smile that mixed innocence and erotic knowledge. "I was waiting for the chapel to empty."

Bill felt his groin jerk in reaction to the warm silk of her voice. In a desperate bid to ignore the spiraling desire he felt, he said weakly, "The church is closed for the night, I'm afraid. I'd be happy to discuss whatever troubles you in the morning, if you wish."

She shook her head. The dark ringlets that framed her face swayed at the slight gesture. "What I want concerns you directly."

"I don't understand." His voice was laced with uncertainty. He'd trained himself to speak in the rich, rolling tones that would carry to every corner of the chapel, but the strong, commanding tone he was trying for sounded flat and flaccid.

"I wished to comfort you," she said. "I can see that you cared for Father Michael a great deal."

"I did. His passing was a great loss to the entire parish and to me, personally. He was my mentor and my friend."

She nodded slowly, one hand coming up to tease at the ebony strands of hair that brushed her cheek. "There is no shame in grieving the loss of a friend. I once aided Father Michael as I would aid you."

Before he could say anything, she lowered her hand and started forward, moving toward him with heedless, predatory grace. Her hips undulated at every step. Her bare feet made no sound on the marble tiles as she stepped out of the light and into the shadow cast by one of the marble and granite columns. Her silhouette was plunged into darkness; only her eyes could be seen clearly, burning out of the gloom like twin lamps.

The shadow relinquished its hold on her with inhuman slowness as her dainty foot appeared. Bill stood transfixed, as every flawless inch of her passed through the moonlight slicing the chapel from a high window. She was a dizzyingly seductive dream made flesh, and although his priest's soul cried out, working against his craving to see more, he could no more turn away than he could deliver his friend's soul to Heaven personally.

A knee appeared, and then another, and where he had remembered fabric, now there was none. Horrified and aroused beyond rational thought, he watched as more of her flesh was laid bare in the moon's spotlight.

Soon her hips appeared, and he realized that his greatest desire and deepest fear had just been realized. The pouting lips of her sex showed clearly through downy wisps of hair, and his mouth went drier still as he stared at her body, revealed with such casual disregard for time or place. Her tiny waist emerged, followed by her full breasts, whose pointed tips seemed to aim at him as malevolently as the barrels of twin guns.

He swallowed, desperate to get some moisture in his mouth so that he could warn her against the sacrilege she was committing. It didn't work; his mouth and throat remained as dry and lifeless as grave dirt. Her hand rose to stroke his cheek, sending a searing wave of forbidden pleasure through his body.

His mind tried to rebel against the attraction, but his body was clearly in charge and refused to listen to the voice in his head whispering of sin and damnation. At this moment, her beauty and her touch were like manna in the desert of his grief.

With the last of his mental strength, just before she pressed herself against him, he cried, "Forgive me Father."

Then her heated mouth touched his, and the priest was lost in a raw storm of need. His arms rose to twine around her as her warmth seeped through the rough gabardine fabric of his priest's clothing. His cock swelled as she molded her body to him.

She tasted of moonlight and dew. His nostrils flared wide to admit the scent of musky night-blooming flowers underlain with the subtle whiff of a burning match head. Her soft, pliant body offered no resistance as he kissed her, finding in her the well that would slake his thirst.

She pulled his shirt loose from his trousers. Deftly, her fingers worked the buttons loose, traveling up his stomach to his chest. Where her fingers touched, a slow, lingering burn remained—a trail of fire that immolated his senses and rendered them more acute all at once.

Her fingers stalled at his Roman collar but he reached up and ripped the offending accessory free of his throat, sloping his shoulders to permit the black shirt to slide down his arms to the floor. Beneath, he wore a plain white undershirt, which she slid over his head, leaving him exposed to the waist.

With a low, appreciative hum, she began to kiss her way up his stomach, punctuating every brush of her lips with a flick of her tongue. Bill groaned with need as her lips seared against his skin, blazing a path up his body to his nipples. Her mouth slipped over them, working her way from one to the other. She bathed his chest avidly until his knees buckled from the sinful wonder of the feeling.

He found himself staring at her sex. Almost against his will, he pressed his face into her, willing her lips to part before his tongue as his arms wrapped around her waist to clutch at his destruction and salvation.

The flavor of her moist pussy was even better than that of her mouth, and he licked her with insatiable hunger and no finesse whatsoever. She didn't seem to mind, arching her hips in a rhythmic dance against his mouth. The damp curls that tickled against his face seemed to pull him inward, and he sucked at her in a frenzy of desire.

She pushed him back, startling him for a moment, before she lay down on the floor and reached up to undo his belt. In short order, his trousers and boxers lay in a dark pool on the floor and she maneuvered between his spread legs to take him in her mouth.

Bill had never experienced anything like it. Masturbation was not unknown to him, and it was the sole indulgence of the flesh he permitted himself. But as her heated, soft mouth took his length into her and the tendrils of her hair played against his thighs, he knew that he would never again be fully satisfied by his own hand. Her tongue played over the swollen head, tickling and teasing at spots he'd never discovered. Her hands moved up to clench lightly around his shaft and his balls, urging him to new heights of ecstasy. He bent to attack her pussy, open and glistening in the moonlight, with renewed vigor until she cried out around a mouthful of his painfully hard cock.

She released her hold on him and moved so that he fell out of her mouth. "Fill me. Take me now!"

Bill could not have resisted had Satan himself appeared at that moment. He moved so that he lay atop her, the head of his cock probing her hot entrance. The contact aroused a hunger beyond any he'd ever known, and he thrust into her as her mouth came up to meet his again.

Her sex sucked at him, taking the entire length of his cock in one smooth, delicious slide. His eyes slid closed as he found his rhythm and began to pound into her liquid heat.

She took his tongue between her teeth, lightly, sucking on it as fervently as she had his cock, and the mingling of pleasure and pain shivered a lightning bolt of furious longing through him. He drove into her ardently, heedless of her comfort or the fact that she lay beneath him on the cold marble floor. His only thought was to plunder and take her, to possess her utterly.

For her part, she met his most ferocious thrusts with lovely gasping cries, her fingernails clawing against his ass as if demanding more of him. She writhed and wriggled against him, throwing her head back as she clamped her inner muscles around him and exploded under him.

Her orgasm triggered his own, and his balls drew up tight against his body as he unleashed a torrent of his own molten release into her fiery depths. His body shuddered and his heart thudded in time with each new spasm.

Finally, spent, he rolled off her to lie panting and exhausted on the floor. The tiles felt like ice against his heated body, but he couldn't be bothered with such insignificant trifles as he gathered her up in his arms and rested his head on her ample bosom.

Just before he drifted off to sleep, he thought he heard her say, "You belong to me, now."

"Father? Father William?"

The high, thin voice of Sister Mary Augustine brought Bill's head up in alarm.

"What is it? What's wrong?"

The nun looked taken aback. "Forgive me, Father, but it's almost breakfast time. We knocked at the rectory, but we couldn't find you. Have you been here all night?"

Bill looked down at himself. To his relief, he was at least decently clad, although his clothing was wrinkled and rumpled from having been slept in. "I suppose I have, Sister," he said slowly. The events of the night before began to play again in his mind, a lustful movie with him in the starring role.

He stood up and pulled his shirt down in a futile attempt to smooth out the wrinkles. Then he ran a hand through his hair as a faint, uneasy chill whispered through him.

"Are you all right, Father?"

Sister Mary Augustine was watching him with eyes that seemed to look right into his soul. Her wizened face wore an expression that suggested that he'd better not even think of trying to sugarcoat what ailed him.

"I had...a very odd dream."

"Humph. You and every other person who's ever stayed the night here," the nun said with finality.

"Have you ever done so?" Bill asked, feeling his heart race a little.

"I have. Once." The nun nodded sharply. "Never after. The dream I had..."

"Tell me more," Bill demanded. The sister's mouth fell open at the whip crack of command that edged his tone. "It may be more important than you know."

"I confessed my sins that night. My conscience is clear." She hedged.

"With all respect, Sister, right now I'm less concerned with the state of your immortal soul than I am in getting to the truth of this matter. Now tell me all."

As the nun spoke, Bill's knees went weak, and he sagged back onto the pew. He could feel the blood draining from his face to pool in his feet, and his head fell forward into his hands.

When she finished, he looked up at her, horrified.

"And no one has reported this?"

"There's been no need, Father. It was a dream, nothing more."

Bill nodded slowly. "I would believe that, except that you and I dreamed of an identical woman. Correct in every particular and detail. Father Michael had told me that there was something I needed to know about this place, but he died before he could relate the information. I suspect this is what he wanted to tell me."

The sister flinched in surprise. "What do you intend to do?"

Bill thought very hard for a moment.

"I don't know yet." His jaw tensed and his eyes narrowed as he considered the ramifications. Finally, he rose to his feet and gathered the full power and authority of his office and, with the sister watching him, he growled, "But before sundown, I will."

THE LONELY HUNTRESS

Mina Murray

She has dreamed of the stranger three times in the past three months, and each time it ends the same: his body looming over her like some dark angel, and then Althea, dissolving. Tonight she dreams of him again, and it is different. His hand is on her breast now, his cock heavy with promise between her thighs, and then he's kissing her and she's dissolving and once again the blackness takes her. Althea wakes to the jungle beat of her own heart.

She moves over to the window, resting her cheek against the cool glass. Her fingertips trace an intricate pattern in the condensation, and she looks out over the city as the 3:00 a.m. rain washes its sins away. The dream's frequency has unsettled her. Dreams have particular significance to her kind, and Althea, the succubus, is trying to shake this dream off. Unsuccessfully. The taut lines of her body betray both her unease and her arousal, and if her small white hand were to slip between her legs in search of release, well, who could blame her? Althea is *hungry*. When she finally returns to bed and drifts off to a dreamless sleep, the name she traced on the windowpane begins to glow.

Tonight Althea hunts again. And she looks forward to it as if it were her first time. For months a kind of nervous energy has been twisting and roiling beneath her skin. Her last hunts have been less than satisfying. She feeds and she enjoys it, but something unnameable has left her feeling tangled up inside afterward, lonely and heartsick and lusting. Over the last two days, a sense of imminence has descended. Something big is brewing, and whatever it is, Althea wants in.

She has dressed for action anyway: those spike-heeled, killer boots; that jade silk dress shifting teasingly over her bare skin. As she walks down the avenue toward the bar, the wind picks up, calling to the rising wildness that makes her want to drink and fuck and dance. *A perfect night for an old-school hunt*, she thinks, *one where I play with my target for hours, then show him my full form, black wings unfurling like some demonic standard*. But Althea had done that once before, and she had paid the price for it. She was not about to risk another decade of exile, not now, when her punishment was almost over. She quickens her pace. Nearly there.

The wave hits her, hard, just before she reaches the arched entryway. She has to pause for a moment to absorb the impact. Her left hand scrabbles for support. Sometimes Althea chooses her prey, and sometimes the instinct chooses for her. This is one of the latter times. Pushing the door open, she makes her way across the room; dim lamps set into sandstone walls send shadows curling around her legs. When she first came into her powers on the eve of her eighteenth birthday, she had to concentrate to separate the tangled threads of everyday energies from the signal that would lead her to her partner for the night, or for the hour. Now, ten years on, it is almost as natural as breathing. Except tonight. For some reason, the signal stutters: now here, then gone.

This is new, she thinks. The uncertainty excites her, fizzes in her blood. The signal tugs at her again, and she turns slowly, as if underwater. Her gaze is drawn to a tall man in a dark suit who walks with a slight hitch in his gait.

Is it him, she wonders? She'll have to get closer to make sure. Maybe touch him. She watches him weave his way through the clusters of people to take a seat at the bar. One beat, then two—mustn't look too eager—and she brushes past him. He orders a rare single malt in a smooth voice. *Oh yes*, she thinks, *he's the one all right*. An image comes to her mind, unbidden, of pushing him up against that wall in the alley outside and kissing him fiercely, branding him, her tongue stroking his, one hand fisted in his hair and the other on his jaw, holding him still for her.

As if he can see into her thoughts, he turns to her, a look on his face like familiarity, or revelation. For the first time in years, Althea blushes.

"Don't I know you from somewhere?" he asks. His eyes survey the curves of her form, unhurried and assured, as if she is already his.

"I don't think so. At least, not yet." She sees her moment and takes it, sliding into the seat next to him with a practiced grace.

"Excellent choice, by the way." She nods at his drink.

"Thank you. I find myself drawn to rare things. One of my weaknesses, I guess." He shrugs. "I'm Lugh, by the way." His handshake is firm, but not too firm.

"Althea." *What warm hands*, she thinks.

"Care to try it?" He proffers his glass. Althea leans in, takes a measured sip. It burns a warm trail down her throat.

"Mm." She licks her lips and is oddly pleased to see him watching her so intently. Things are moving faster than she anticipated. Her pulse starts to throb, keeping time with the music. She feels the beat all through her body, needs to move.

"Would you like to dance?" She has forgotten about his mild limp, and though he seems taken aback he recovers quickly, downs the rest of his whisky.

"Sure."

Her skin jumps as he brushes his palm down her bare arm. There's some dirty funk playing, perfect for close contact. Soon she's pressed back against him, her arms around his neck. Her hips circle and shift, grinding into his growing hardness. His hands stroke up and down the sides of her body. She feels his lips on her throat, his breath in her ear as he whispers: "My place. Around the corner. Let's go. Please."

It's the "please" that sets her clit twitching.

They barely make it inside before he is on her, his jacket hastily tossed aside. In reverse mimicry of her earlier fantasy, it is Althea who is now overcome. He threads his hands through her long black hair and pulls, opening her throat to him.

"So beautiful," Lugh murmurs, "so vulnerable."

Althea sees the white flash of his teeth before he bites her neck. He presses her arms above her head, crosses them at the wrists, holds them there with the one strong hand while he grips her jaw with the other and tilts her head up and back. *This is it,* she thinks, *this is it.*

Lugh's kiss is not gentle, but then she doesn't want it to be. It is possessive, all-consuming. He bites her pouty lower lip, retreats, advances, strokes her tongue with his. She moans into his mouth, bites him back, and then he breaks the kiss. She looks at him, bereft, and he laughs softly.

Althea is still pinned against the stuccoed wall, and she real-izes, with a start, that she has lost control of this encounter, and oh, how fast. She has no idea what he will do next. *What is this?* she wonders. *Surrender?*

As he kicks her legs apart, a quiet voice inside her answers *Yes*. All those years being the architect of someone else's plea-sure have led her here. For once she wants to feel as her prey does, helpless to resist in the face of a greater force. But Althea is not used to being the one who gives it up. Even as her body swells toward him, she fights Lugh's iron grip.

"Let me," he whispers, sensing her anxiety, but still not releasing her. "Let me, it will be good, I promise."

Althea whimpers as his hand disappears under her dress. He does not bother removing her revealing scrap of underwear, merely pulls it to one side as he slides a finger into her, discov-ering her wet heat. He works her slickness up over that little pearl of hers, feels her spasm beneath his hand.

"So sweet, Althea, you are so fucking sweet." He kisses her roughly, his brown hair falling forward, over her forehead. "I'm going to let go of your wrists, but you're going to keep your arms up for me, aren't you?"

Althea nods mutely.

With his other hand now freed, he drops to his knees, pulls her panties off, spreads her legs wider. His fingers draw circles on her clit, her cunt clamps around the second of his fingers to enter her. There is a look of triumph on Lugh's handsome face.

As she undulates against him—she is so close—his green eyes seem to flare brightly. *Weren't they brown before?* She can't remember. She can't bring herself to care. She is coming, and the pleasure is so intense it is almost too much, and suddenly Althea finds she does not mind surrender. No, she does not mind it at all.

When she finally looks up at him, she is surprised by her own reticence. *What kind of a succubus am I, standing here like some blushing virgin?* Lugh steps forward, strokes her cheek lightly, moves to undress her properly.

"No," she says, trying to regain her equilibrium. "No, I'll do it."

She strips out of her dress as Lugh's gaze burns brighter and saunters over to him, exaggerating the sway of her hips. "Now it's your turn."

Lugh whips off his white shirt, and then plays it coy, unbuttoning his pants in ultraslow motion. His skin gleams golden in the lamplight, and Althea's eyes widen as she takes in the tribal tattoos that curl over his arms and torso like snakes, and the gold loop piercing his left nipple. The wildness under his suit excites her like nothing else has in a long time. She loves peeling back the layers of someone and seeing something unexpected. Lugh does not, will not, disappoint.

She reaches out to trace the subtle architecture of veins along his arms. The outlines of his ink seem to shift, impossibly, under her touch.

"Lugh," she asks, pulling back, "these tattoos—where did you get them?"

There is a strange expression on his face; she cannot parse its meaning.

"Why do you ask?"

"They just feel—okay, this is going to sound crazy—they just feel alive, I guess."

"Of course they're alive," he says, then kisses her wrist. "They move when I do, when my skin does, when my pulse beats beneath them."

He knows that is not what she meant.

He guides her palm to his cock, and the size of his erection, the evidence of his desire for her, drives all rational thought from her head. She looks down, entranced by the way her fingers curl around him. The pad of her forefinger rubs over the dusky crown, shiny with a crystalline tear of precum.

"Now that you've looked your fill," he growls, "you're going to follow me, and I'm going to fuck you in my bed."

When Lugh pushes her onto her back and straddles her chest, she rubs her face against his satiny skin and inhales deeply. Althea as a rule had always left the act of feeding to the very end, to those final moments when her partner found bliss. The trade-off seemed right, somehow. Tonight she breaks her rule. Each time she sucks Lugh's cock into her pretty mouth she takes a little of his energy into her. And he is strong. Stronger than anyone she's ever had. She'll have to be careful not to take too much, too soon. Althea has only ever killed a partner once. She pulls off him just before he is about to come, before the taste of him can fall on her tongue like a benediction.

"I thought you were going to fuck me."

There is a challenge in her voice and he answers it.

Something primal flashes behind his eyes and he moves faster than he should be able to. Before she knows it, she is beneath him and her legs are spread so wide it is almost the wrong side of painful. His fingers bite into her inner thighs and she knows there'll be bruises tomorrow. But a hand is at her breast now, caressing it, plucking delicately at her nipple, and when he finally enters her it is fluid and slow and sweet.

I never knew it could be like this, she thinks, *both battle and tenderness*. His hips cant forward, and he starts to thrust; short, teasing strokes at first.

Althea arches up to meet him, and Lugh groans. She is so wet, so welcoming, but he can't get deep enough inside her.

"Sit up," he rasps. "Wrap your legs around me." She hops up

on top of him, and her eyes search his for something she doesn't yet know she wants. Communion? Oblivion? She presses her lips to his and draws his energy into her again.

Lugh's hands close on her hips, guide her down onto him. Althea throws her head back and cries out when his cock hits that sweet spot deep inside her. She writhes on him like the wild thing she is.

"Fuck, Lugh, fuck. You have the face of an angel, but you sure fuck like a demon."

His low laugh vibrates through them both. There is an odd edge to it, but Althea doesn't notice that. She is too busy turning tight circles with her hips, rubbing her clit on the base of his cock.

"Markus," he says, between thrusts. "Call me Markus."

"But your name is Lugh."

He begins to pull out of her, even as she clings to him.

"Please," he begs, "please, just call me Markus."

She is so desperate for him now, so fuck-drunk, that she would call him any name under the sun, any name he asked her to.

"Fine," she gasps, "Markus."

He looks at her, something ritual in his gaze.

"Take me inside you, Althea. Take me inside you now."

"Please. Markus, please. I want you, I want all of you." She lowers herself down onto him, cunt-deep in bliss. He grips her hands, laces his fingers through hers. The unexpected intimacy makes her heart clench, and they push against each other, striving toward ecstasy. A rosy flush starts to color her neck. The spike in his energy signal tells her just how close he is too.

"Look at me, Althea, look at me."

She starts to come at the same time as he does, his green-eyed gaze raking her face, and then she is dissolving, just like in her dream. But this time there is no fear, and when the blackness comes it claims her like a lover.

The next day she wakes, alone, in her own bed. Her dress is draped neatly over the armchair in the corner of her room. She pauses on her way to the bathroom to hang it up, trying to remember how she got home.

I didn't have that much to drink, she thinks, reaching for a glass of water.

When Althea catches a glimpse of her reflection in the mirror, she drops the glass. Along the left side of her body are tattoos, and standing beside her is a man she has never met in the flesh. The tattoos adorning the right side of his torso and the length of his right arm flicker as if alive. Althea notices that they join up perfectly to hers.

They are Lugh's tattoos, she remembers. This is not Lugh, though. Where Lugh's hair was brown, the stranger's is black. Lugh's skin was tanned; this man's is pale. But she knows this man's face: it has followed her in her dreams for months. She knows his green eyes too.

"Markus?"

Althea takes a deep breath, tries to tamp down the panic.

"Okay, explain to me exactly what the fuck is going on. What *are* you?"

She sees his lips move. No sound comes out, but she can hear him anyway. "You know what I am, Althea."

She knows the word before she can speak it.

"Incubus."

"We're the same," he says, "the same kind. I just don't have my physical body anymore."

And then the dreams make sense to her.

"You've been calling to me for months, haven't you?" She

doesn't need him to answer, but he nods anyway.

"I need one of my own kind to host me, to sustain me until I can find a way back to my own body. Lugh was only human, and humans aren't strong enough. I've jumped from body to body for the last six months." His face is grave. "I don't want to kill, Althea, but I don't want to die either."

"So, last night, when we…"

"Yes," Markus nods. "When you said my true name, you accepted me into you."

"Can I force you out?"

"It would kill me, but yes." He pauses for a moment. "Don't worry, I can't take away your will, or make you do anything you don't want to. But there are things I can do for you, things I *would* do for you, as payment. You'll be stronger with me, for one; I can protect you from harm. Look down."

The shards of broken glass have fallen around her feet in an impossibly perfect circle.

"And you won't be lonely anymore."

A single tear slides down her cheek. Markus catches it on his fingertip.

"There are other things I can do for you too," he says, his voice gentle. "Will you let me show you?"

She nods.

His reflection begins to merge with hers, and Althea feels him slipping into the spaces that keep them apart. A hand skims lovingly down to her sex. It feels like a stranger's hand. No, not a stranger's hand. Markus's hand.

Althea is home at last.

NEITHER LOVE
NOR MONEY

Giselle Renarde

How's Bernadetta feeling these days?"

Jean leaned over the low side of Max's cubicle, wearing that familiar pouty-sad smile all the female staff put on when they passed his workspace. *Since when do you care how she's feeling? Max wanted to say. You deride Detta more than anyone!*

But, "Same as always," was all he said.

Max only held his tongue because Jean was holding a huge tub of chocolate peanut butter ice cream. As much as he loved Bernadetta, and he did with all his heart, he wanted a damn bowl! The three o'clock lull had hit and it took a sugar rush to make it through the day.

When an offer was not forthcoming, Max asked, "What have you got there, Jean?"

The creases around her gray eyes multiplied as she smiled super-sweetly. "Oh, I made poor Bernadetta a batch of chicken noodle soup, my grandmother's recipe. Should lift her spirits some."

"Oh." Max had to admit, he was disappointed there would be no ice cream, but he couldn't deny how kind a gesture this was. "Well, thank you very much, Jean. I'm sure she'll appreciate it."

Carrying the damn thing home by subway without spilling it all over somebody's fine Italian shoes wasn't easy, but nothing in his relationship with their company's figurehead had ever been easy. Bernadetta always liked to remind the staff that she'd built Detta Designs from the ground up, and everything they did, good or bad, was a direct reflection on her. The women who worked for her were ruthlessly jealous. Detta was so goddamn beautiful they told themselves, and anyone else who would listen, that she'd slept her way to the top.

And, in a sense, that was true. But not in the way women like Jean were thinking.

"Honey, I'm home!" Max called out as he stepped into her ornate condo apartment. Bernadetta was rich enough to buy one of those McMansions just outside the city, but she preferred to have her finger on the pulse. She also could have afforded private nursing staff during the day so Max wouldn't have to worry so much, but most healthcare workers wouldn't understand.

"Have a nice day at the office, sweetheart?" She looked weak, a shadow of her formerly vivacious self, lying there under fourteen blankets she'd probably kick off in five seconds anyway. Hot to cold, she went hot to cold—sweating to freezing.

Max put on a brave smile, despite feeling wretchedly helpless. "Not bad. Jean made you some soup." He held up the ice-cream tub.

Tilting her sallow cheek weakly against her pillow, she let out a feeble laugh and asked, "Chocolate peanut butter soup? Sounds delicious."

Her effort made him smile. "It's chicken noodle, apparently."

He checked on her five times while he heated it up. Her dark hair, once so thick and lustrous, had started falling out, and her hands looked skeletal. Her face did, too, so much so that Max found himself trying not to look at her.

When she'd first hired him, Max couldn't look Bernadette in the eye because her beauty so overwhelmed him. She'd been the source of hundreds of instant erections, back then. All she had to do was saunter by his cubicle and—bing!—he was stiff as a telephone pole. How many hard-ons had he rubbed out in the end stall of the men's room? He'd lost count.

What is it about her? he'd wondered, back then—back before he knew. It was everything: the long hair, the long legs, the round ass under those tight leather skirts, big tits bursting out of matching jackets, only the thin ruffle of some see-through blouse separating her pale white skin from her thin lapels. God, he wanted to bury his face in her cleavage. There was just so goddamn much of it! And the way her tits were all pressed together like that, revealing so much flesh, he was always sure she might bend far enough for them to cascade into full view.

And those were just the tangibles. There was something in her eyes, when he actually brought himself to look into them, that was both mesmerizing and terribly, terribly frightening. A man could lose himself in those eyes. He got the feeling many men had, given the way she'd stare at him unsmilingly, then allow a slow grin to bleed across those crimson lips. Many men were lost somewhere inside of her.

Thinking back, it was one of those typical working-late-with-the-boss situations when he discovered Bernadetta's true nature. And when he found out—when he *realized* what she was—everything fell into place.

Max had always been good with visuals. They were putting together the next year's catalogue, and Detta's office was strewn with boards of glossy pictures and panels of text. She'd asked for his help, for his "eye" as she put it. He'd always wondered if she meant for this to happen, for any of it to happen, or if it was all some kind of near-fatal accident.

He was bending over the sideboard at the time, in part to get a closer look at the mock-ups propped against the wall, in part to conceal his massive erection. She'd come up behind him, so close he could feel the heat of her front against his ass. That heat only got him harder, and his dick slapped the edge of the sideboard, begging for something soft, something hot. Then rough. And he knew that was exactly what he'd get from Bernadetta.

Grabbing his sides with two strong hands, she'd dug her blood-red nails into his flesh and bucked her hips against his ass, like she could fuck him that way. In that moment, he wished she could. He wanted her to take him, just strip him bare and do whatever the hell she wanted with his body. He'd be hers if she wanted him. He'd give her anything.

Did she turn him around or did he do that himself? Somehow he ended up facing her, and she tore off his tie with one hand while she found his hard cock with the other. How did she manage to zero in like that? Just wham! She had it in her fist, stroking hard through the fabric.

Max knew she wouldn't be gentle. He could see it in her, right from the start. She manhandled him, so strong, so tough, nearly his height in those fuck-me heels. When she let go of his cock, it was only to tie his wrists behind him with his own goddamn tie. She pressed him back against the sideboard, and he was afraid he might ruin one of the catalogue mock-ups, but if she didn't care why should he? So he pressed his head back against the glossy board while Bernadetta tore open his shirt.

Buttons went flying, falling to the floor in slow motion, each one a mother-of-pearl drop of rain settling on the industrial office carpet. He was so mesmerized by the subtle shimmer that he almost didn't notice Detta ripping his belt from its loops. She tossed it around her shoulders and, in his eyes, it morphed into a sleek black snake hissing curiously while his boss opened his fly. His pants dropped to the floor with the weight of his wallet in the back pocket and his keys in the front.

"Oh, my god." Max didn't think he could speak, but the words came out again when she pushed his jockeys down his thigh. "Oh, my fucking god." His cock sprang up to whack his naked belly, and the cool air was almost a relief against the blazing heat of his erection.

Bernadetta didn't respond, didn't even look up at him as she grasped his hard dick, pumping it in her fist. He was more turned on than he'd ever been in all his life as he watched his thick purplish cockhead spilling streams of precum across his boss's fingers. For a moment, he worried he'd be in trouble, maybe lose his job, but Bernadetta answered his unspoken concern with a kiss so powerful it sent every ounce of his energy between his legs.

Her mouth was sweltering, sizzling, and when her tongue battled his, he fought hard but lost miserably. There was no winning with Bernadetta. She was too strong, too commanding, too unyielding, to truly contend with. Max knew instinctively that they were not on a level playing field.

And yet it was Bernadetta who leaned down, bending at the hips, scratching his bare chest all the way down, until the pads of her fingers pressed into his pubic hair. His hips bucked uncontrollably when she touched him there, touched his pelvis, slipped those fingers down to cup his balls. He hissed, then, with the sensation. God, she was rough and it hurt, the way she grabbed them, the way she squeezed. The pain was brilliant.

Slipping his belt from around her shoulders, she wrapped it around Max's thighs, low down, almost at his knees. He watched in disbelief as she pulled the braided leather taut, so tight around his legs the belt dug into his skin. Sucking cool air in through his teeth, he splayed his palms flat on the sturdy wooden sideboard. Until this moment, he'd never felt so wonderfully endangered in Bernadetta's office.

He couldn't move. He knew that now. Though his position, leaning back, wrists secured behind him, legs bound tight, wasn't precarious in itself, Max felt that if he budged even slightly in any direction, he'd lose his balance. The haze of the situation was beginning to take over, and the edges of reality seemed to bleed into something fantastical, something dizzy and delightful, but with an unshakable, dark underbelly. Something was happening now. Something that had never happened to Max before....

"Bernadetta?" His head hung low, swinging side to side as she tossed that long stream of dark hair over one shoulder. The snake was back, black, hissing, squeezing his legs so tight he felt choked by it.

And then another snake, a pink one, velvet, was tickling the slit of his cockhead. Her tongue. Her hot, wet, slithering, writhing tongue traced a slick circle around his tip and he shuddered with the pleasure of her mouth. If he'd been able to move, he would have bucked forward, forced himself between those lips, but he couldn't budge. He was stuck, and dizzy besides. He couldn't keep his head up any longer. He tried to lift it, but it was too damn heavy.

Slumping forward, he watched those crimson lips part. Bernadetta's face was a blur of green eyes and red lipstick on a pale white canvas. Her nose, cheekbones, all her features disappeared as she swallowed him whole, honest-to-god deep-throating his cock, right to the root. He'd never experienced anything like it, and he held his breath to keep from losing the moment: her hot mouth enveloping his shaft, her warm breath rustling his pubic hair, her hand cupping his balls mercilessly.

And then, at an absolutely torturous speed, she leaned back, leaned away and very nearly let his cock fall from her mouth. But not quite. She held him there between her lips, sucking just the tip before swallowing him all over again. Faster this time. Faster the next, until it became an in-and-out, a game, a race. He didn't know how she managed to stay in that position, legs perfectly straight in those killer heels, bending only at the hips, head tilted so he got a good view of her face. She sucked him hard. It was the sweetest torment conceivable, but what could he do? He so wanted to thrust forward to drive the monster she had enticed even faster and deeper but something held him in place, something more than the physical restraints. He belonged to her in every sense.

Max wouldn't last long like this, but when his eyelids started to droop, feeling heavy as his head, he worried a bit. She kept sucking, but he couldn't watch. He couldn't see. He tried to shift his weight to his hands so he could raise his hips just a touch, but it was useless. His muscles had once been thick ropes. Now they felt like dental floss. Despite his arousal, despite his desire to fill his boss's mouth with cum, his body was kitten-weak. Couldn't he just lie down? On the carpet would be fine. He didn't mind. Just lie down, just a little rest...

Bernadetta sucked him hard, now pumping his shaft with one hand, squeezing his balls with the other. Max felt a telltale trembling in his thighs, a quaking in his balls, but it was all so far away, like he was feeling somebody else's orgasm. His cum flooded her mouth, he felt that much, but the first surge sent him hurdling psychically backward, like the recoil on a pistol. Darkness consumed his peripheral vision. All he could see before him was the whiteness of Bernadetta's face.

The shots kept firing, jizz streaming from his cock to her mouth, sending him back even farther into the darkness. Farther and farther still. Until everything was in shadow. Darkness all around. Nothing else.

He'd woken up in the very bed Detta presently occupied, probably looking a hell of a lot like she did right now. Over the hazy days that followed, as she'd nursed him back to health, she'd confessed her nature to him. In that strange dream-like state, it made perfect sense that Detta should be a succubus. Why not? Hell, it hadn't even fazed him when she admitted she could steal his essence in its entirety, but wouldn't because she'd found that she loved Max too much. This had never happened before, never in her life. She really and truly loved him.

Max approached the bed with a bowl of Jean's soup on a tray. His heart fell when he caught sight of the succubus he loved slumped on her pillow, fragile and weak.

"Detta," he said, and she looked up at him. His fingers tightened around the sides of the tray. "You can't go on like this. Just take what you need from me."

She looked up at him softly, a glaze filling her eyes. "But I love you, Max." That's what she always said. "I can't impose this life on you anymore. Trust me, it's not as fun as it looks." She smiled meekly. "And I can't take the force from strangers, the way I used to, because..." *Cough. Wheeze.* "Because I've realized, Max, that everybody out there has someone who loves them the way I love you. How could I take that away? How could I take it from anybody?"

"A repentant succubus," Max chuckled. Sitting beside her on the bed, he placed the soup tray on her night table. "Now there's something you don't see every day." He rested another pillow behind her head before spooning soup between her pale, drawn lips.

"It's good," she said. "Thank Jean for me?"

Max watched as a blush of color returned to Detta's cheeks and lips. She'd always been pale, but there was a vitality missing these days. He knew what she needed from him, but would she ever just swallow her pride and take what he was willing to give?

Shifting the blankets aside, Max found Bernadetta naked underneath. She must have cast off her nightgown during one of her fever sweats. When he closed his eyes, he saw her body as it once was, and as it could be again: full and fleshy, bouncing and bountiful. He could give her that.

"Don't you think I love you too?" He traced his tongue down her chest, so deliciously salty with sweat, and stopped only when he arrived at her pert nipple.

When he sucked it, Detta's chest bucked and she gasped. "What are you doing, Max?"

He answered her question with one of his own: "Don't you think I would do anything for you? Don't you think I'd give you everything I have to give?"

"Please," she whispered, though she was panting with familiar lust as he kissed a path down her sallow belly. "I don't want to lose you."

"I don't want to lose you! Let's just get you a little stronger, then I'm sure we can find you other ways of feeding. We'll figure something out, Detta. Just, please, let me help you."

She cried out when the tip of his tongue met her pink folds. Her clit was hiding, but he found it. If he could get her started like this, surely she'd find enough energy to take from him what she needed. He just had to turn her on first—and judging by her hoarse moans, he was certainly accomplishing that much.

Her pussy was getting wet now, whether with his saliva or her juices Max wasn't entirely sure, but he lapped the strong flavor from her lips. She whimpered when he sucked her clit. God, she was getting there—he could feel it! He had the power to get her there, and he worked hard at it. Damned if he wouldn't hear her screaming for mercy, her thin frame shuddering against the mattress, her pussy quaking under his tongue.

"Max!" she cried. "Max..."

When he looked up, he realized Bernadetta was waving her hand in a come-hither motion. At first, he wasn't sure what she meant. And then she licked her lips, and they looked full once again, glossy and plump and deep, deep red.

"Get up here," she said with a giving smile. "I want you in my mouth."

They were the greatest words of affection Max had ever heard, and as she wrapped those perfect lips around the head of his cock, sucking resolutely, all he could think to say was, "I love you, Detta."

TEXTUAL

Robin Tiergarten

It started with a text message: *I want you.*

Hayden read it, checked the number and didn't recognize it. He was hoping it was from Rachael, a woman with whom he had dinner last night. It wasn't her number, so he ignored it.

Later in the afternoon, he received another text that read: *I must have you.* It was from the same number. He figured it was someone sending a lover a message. He ignored it. He was talking to a friend at a coffee shop. He wasn't concerned.

The next one read: *I'll change your life.*

He smiled at that one. It seemed a bit egotistical. He was glad he wasn't dating this woman (or man) because frankly the message seemed narcissistic. How full of it could you get? Change his life? Hayden doubted it.

Thankfully, he was meeting Frieda after work. They'd meet at the bar across from her office. It was simple and fun. Sometimes they pretended they didn't know each other. He'd pretend to pick her up for a night of wild sex. The play made for fun, but now Frieda was late. And frankly, he knew she cared more about her work than any relationship with him. He had been thinking of ending it for a while. He finished his beer while he waited. Then a text came from Frieda. It said she would be at least forty-five more minutes. He ordered another beer and watched playoff baseball.

His phone beeped. The screen read *new message*. He clicked on *READ*.

It said: *I see you. I definitely want you.*

He stared at the phone's screen for a second, found the number was the same as the messages from earlier in the day and decided he would play the game—at least for forty-five minutes. Perhaps it was Frieda with a new phone and a new dedication toward their relationship. It was unlikely, but Hayden reasoned that you never knew what a person would do.

He scanned the crowded bar, trying to figure out who could have sent the text. Four women seemed possible. A blonde pretended not to look at him and then made a few glances his way. *Nah,* he thought, *not the right attitude.* A brunette made eye contact, but then her date returned with drinks. A dark Latina smiled when his eyes fell on her, but she could not be the woman because she seemed much too shy when she broke eye contact, looked into her drink and would not look at him again. The last possibility was a black-haired woman who sat alone at a small table.

Another text came in: *Not her. I'll send you a clue.*

Hayden smiled. This was fun. He wondered where she was.

A picture message arrived. He opened it. A picture of a green dress pulled up and black panties pulled down stared up at him. In the center was a pussy with a small tuft of red pubes. It looked good—tight, trim and wet.

Redhead! He searched the bar. No sign anywhere. No redhead.

Another text: *You like? Text back.*

What the hell? Hayden thought. *I am curious and interested.*

He typed: *Definitely like. Where are you?*

The response: *Not in the bar.*

How do you know I'm in a bar?

Think you have been alone all day? I decided I wanted you. I pursue what I want. I've been tailing you. Like my tail enough? Then come outside.

He stared at the screen. Then he looked at the picture again. He liked what he saw. Her pussy was stunning. He decided he wanted her as well.

He typed: *Be right there.*

He walked out of the crowded bar. The street outside was not exactly bustling. No redhead waited outside. He looked at the parked cars. He saw no redhead.

Another picture message came.

This time a woman's breasts heaved out of a dress. They were pert, full and topped with perfectly sized aureolae and tight small nipples—just the way he liked them.

The message below them read: *Waiting for a squeeze. Come satisfy me.*

He wrote back: *Lovely. Please tell me where you are.*

The screen read: *If I do, I expect my treat. Will you give me what I want?*

His reply: *Tell me what you want.*

He read: *I want YOU. Completely, all of you. Every inch. Will you give that to me?*

As he finished reading the text his phone beeped. A picture message waited to be opened. She was fast. He opened it. When he did, he saw something out of focus. It was clearly flesh, but he couldn't quite make out what it was. Still, it had a fuzzy, erotic quality about it. Something that pulled him forward, made him feel it in his body.

He replied: *Yes.*

He waited. It took a few more seconds before his screen notified him of a new message: *Stay where you are. I'll be right there.*

A few minutes later a black limo slowed and pulled up beside him. The back window slid down. A woman with shoulder-length red hair, fair skin, green eyes and absolutely stunning glossy red lips called his name.

"Ready for a ride?" she asked. She opened the door. When she did, he took in her stunning body draped in a green dress. She was beyond anything he could have anticipated. He felt as if he had entered a dream. Why him? Fuck it. Who cared!

"Hurry."

He climbed in and sat on the black leather seat beside her. He looked around. The privacy glass between the driver and their seat was up. It was not just smoked; it was completely black. Here they were in a private compartment.

"Wine?" she asked, holding out a glass of red.

"Thank you."

He took it and sipped. It was delicious.

The limo pulled away.

"Tell me how you knew I was in the bar and what I was doing."

"Intuition."

"Sure."

"That and my assistants."

"Assistants?"

"Call them helpers if you like. I have plenty of them. The one in the bar was helpful. He's trustworthy. But they all are, even the one backing him up."

"So you're just doing this for kicks because you are rich and bored."

"Something like that." She sipped her wine and looked at the tinted window for a moment. Then she returned to him. "You'll like it. Trust me. You're made for it. Perfect for it."

Hayden shrugged. This woman was definitely something else, but she was amazingly attractive and something about her pulled on his bones and flesh.

"Where are we going?"

"We're going to a special place, Hayden."

He asked how she knew his name. It seemed fantastic, but she said she had found him online. She picked him because of his interests. Her online search had shown her that. She claimed she knew what he liked and how he liked it. It was all there online in the text and pictures. All of it was there if you knew how to read between the lines.

"And what do I like?"

"You like intense rough sex—oral, vaginal, anal. And you like to be controlled. You like it when a woman takes command. You like to be a servant, a slave, a sexual tool. You want someone who knows that about you. Someone who knows how to use you properly." She smiled. "How's that?"

He said nothing.

Their eyes locked. Neither said a word. Her eyes glowed with a strange light, but perhaps it was just the streetlights as the limo picked up speed. Her tongue found the corner of her mouth.

"It's time."

She pulled up her dress and spread her legs.

"Go on."

Hayden dropped to the limo floor and positioned himself between her legs. There it was. Exactly like the photo, he thought. No, better. As he moved closer, he breathed her in. She was earthy and humid. The primal smell, something that really had no comparison, worked right through him. It traveled through his nostrils, exploded in his brain, streaked down his spine and surged in his cock. He grew erect before his lips and mouth touched her.

She tasted good. No, that wasn't it. She tasted better than anyone he'd ever tasted before. There was no artificial scent, nothing to get in the way of her pure moisture as it collected on her. And there was something unusual in it, something not of this earth, something like perfectly ripe plums on a summer day. It burst from her labia as he licked and nibbled. He had to have more.

He drove his tongue into her, dipping into her flowing wetness until the flavor exploded in his mouth. And he ate greedily.

She wrapped her fingers through his hair and forced his head even closer. His nose and cheek pushed against her soaking labia.

He couldn't breathe but he drove his tongue in deeper. As he struggled for breath, she rode him, shifting her hips back and forth.

Then she pulled him back. He sucked in a breath and let out a moan. She pulled his hair, leading him downward. His tongue found her tight round hole. He licked and played at the entrance. The taste was as good and primal as her pussy. Her moisture was everywhere. His face was soaked; her flesh was soaked. He felt bathed in her. It made him desire even more. He pushed his tongue inside her round hole, slowly at first, pulling it out and then working it in deeper and deeper. Soon his tongue was buried in her ass as deeply as it had been in her pussy. She forced his face against her flesh, buried him deeply. His nose was at her pussy's entrance; she pushed her hips at him, making the tip move just slightly inside.

She moaned as she rode his face, grinding on it with pleasure. She shuddered and pushed him as deeply as she could.

Then she pulled him away. She released his hair and reclined
on the black leather seat. Her legs spread open. Her scent filled
the small compartment. She was an exotic flower in a hothouse.
The tinted windows were fogged.

Hayden pulled his pants from his body. She grabbed his cock
and pulled him toward her. Without a word, he penetrated her.
She drove her nails into his ass as he pumped into her. Over and
over, she raked his back with her nails. He drove himself into
her and stared into eyes that seemed to burn with unearthly
fire. She brought her bloody nails to her mouth and licked them
while he fucked her. She scratched his shoulder and chest while
he fucked her. When he was on the verge of coming, she pushed
him back.

"I want all of you. Do I get it?"

"Yes."

"Then I'll take what I want."

She thrust her hand against his chest. He felt something stir
inside and get pulled toward the surface.

"Now fuck me. Fill me so I can enjoy all of you."

He felt the pulling at his chest where her hand pressed, felt
her pussy tighten on him, felt himself ejaculating.

She moaned as he did, riding his thrusting cock.

He watched as she pulled her hand away from his chest.
With it came something smoky, nearly immaterial. It looked
like a small version of himself.

What the fuck?

She brought the wisp to her face and sucked it in, taking
the ghostly Hayden between her lips and clamping them shut.
When she did, she shuddered in waves of pleasure.

* * *

Hayden watched the tall blond man at the bar. The man read his phone. Hayden knew exactly what he would do next. Sure enough, the man scanned the room looking for the woman who had just sent him the pussy picture. Hayden knew exactly what would happen next. He'd send the man another text. Then he'd send the tit picture. He knew how it would all play out: a trip in the damned limo, a good fucking or whatever the man desired and the master would take him just as Hayden himself had been taken. It's just a little thing that gets her off, just a little immaterial thing. To her, a soul was pleasure; to a human, a soul was something more.

He was glad he didn't have to drive the limo and see that moment. Still some things continued to haunt him even three years later. For example, he pitied the man when it was over and he looked at the phone again. He knew the man would see the blurry picture in full focus, knew he'd see her true face—what she really was.

SUCCUMB

Cynthia Rayne

H ow deliciously adorable.

The boy thought *he* was hunting *me*. Most mortal men can sense that I'm a sexual predator, not the prey, but college boy didn't seem to perceive the danger. Excellent. I hadn't had a young one in a very long time and truthfully, I deserved the treat. They could stay hard and eager for such a long time and admittedly, I was famished.

Always so very hungry. The curse of my kind.

I smiled at him, slyly, teasingly. We were seated at separate tables at a pub in Philly. I love the old brick and the slightly damp smell. I've been patronizing the Horse and Horn since the revolution, in different guises, of course. Lovely thing about my powers: I can change from supermodel to old crone or anything in between without much effort. And tonight? Full moon, autumn chill in the air—it felt like a redhead kind of evening.

The brash boy grinned at me and walked over with a cocky swagger that made me wet. Another curse of my kind. Always wet and hungry, eager for another feeding.

"What is a beautiful woman like you doing alone?" He flipped the chair around, a scrape of steel against the wooden floor, and straddled it.

"Waiting for the right kind of man to keep me company. And I do enjoy company." I've learned to bait my trap very well. I hinted at decadent bedroom delights but was just a little coy. Mortal men enjoyed a bit of chase, before *I* finally caught them.

He had a quirky little grin. "Cool. What's your name?"

Cool? Yes, now I remembered why I'd gone after older prey. "Victoria. What's yours?" I purred the last bit and made eye contact just a shade too long. Powerful thing, eye contact. I can ensnare a man with my gaze, but that's rather like shooting fish in the proverbial barrel. Where's the challenge?

"I'm Brad. Nice to meet you, Victoria. Have a boyfriend?"

I shook my head. While I have known many, many men, none of them has been my boyfriend. Or even my friend for that matter.

My foolish paramours have been nothing more than a series of appetizers to me. None have quenched my molten need. None could put that fire out. So I use their bodies to buy me temporary respite from the insatiable need. But something about Brad melted me a little.

I loved the way he stared at me with that boyish smile—and boy swagger. Who knew?

He continued to watch me, his face full of wonder and... curiosity. "You aren't what you seem, are you?"

Suddenly I was a girl in a bar once more—this bar, in fact. It was just like the night another immortal had gotten his fix with *me*. Took my virtue and my innocence and gave me eternity, with an unending hunger.

James had played with me for weeks. I knew he was a cad. Knew that he had bedded his way through every tavern in Philadelphia. People talked. But I didn't care. He was handsome. Black hair and green eyes. Hard, horseman's body.

He'd teased me for weeks. Fanny had been my mortal name and he had called me feckless Fanny, breaking men's hearts. Whispered in my ears and brought me meaningless trinkets. He'd taken me out behind the pub and had me against a dirty stone wall. America had been on the edge of a revolution when he had taken my mortality and saddled me with the yearning for fleshy delights.

I had no idea, when he sank his John Thomas in me, he would drain my life force, my very soul. I woke up the next morning, stronger than I had been before. And eager—very eager.

I vowed then and there I would never have more than a one-night stand, I would never drain them, and I would never make another. James had said I was too pretty a miss to be Death's date. He'd whispered that as he'd fucked me. I often wish he had killed me.

But now I stared into Brad's eyes, and I wanted him. My hunger wouldn't be denied.

A short time later, we strolled to my apartment in the shadow of the Horse and Horn. I closed the door and tossed my jacket on the counter. I slid the straps of my dress down and shimmied out. No bra. Panties would be painful. Just bare skin. I had lost my inhibitions along with mortal life.

Brad groaned and reached for me. I sucked at his mouth, devouring with my tongue. I threaded my hands through his hair and pulled his head back. "Brad, I want you to fuck me. Hard."

Brad gasped. I could see his cock distending his jeans, pulsing and eager. "Christ, you're killing me."

I grinned. Really, he had no idea.

Reaching for his belt, I undid it and then unzipped his fly. I pushed his pants, along with his shorts, down his thighs, and his hard cock fell into my hands. I stroked it, relishing the way he closed his eyes, rolled his hips. The tip was capped with precum. I rubbed my thumb over it.

"Brad, I need you to fuck me." I bent over the couch and raised my hips. I felt Brad behind me, his cock at my entrance, the weight of his balls. He slid in. Contact. And a wave slid through me. I came immediately. I loved the friction, the motion of being fucked. My body kneaded his cock, milking him, and his essence poured into me again and again. Along with his life force. Just a little bit. Just enough to tide me over. After I'd drawn four orgasms from him, he collapsed to his knees and I lay on the couch sprawled on my tummy.

I'm not sure when he carried me to bed. I lay curled on my side of the bed with him lying next to me, his face covered in shadow. I leaned in against his human warmth and shut my eyes, if only to pretend for a brief moment I wasn't alone.

"You are so beautiful."

It had been so long since I'd had a genuine compliment, a comment that expressed admiration, rather than a move calculated to get me into bed. I am well versed in seduction. I have slept with everyone, from politicians and lawyers to tailors and famous chefs. My nest is feathered quite well. Essential oils, erotic toys, silk sheets...

But I was ultimately alone. Lonely. And for now, being in the arms of boyish Brad felt good. I could pretend to be human, if only for a moment. But this was dangerous. Far more dangerous. I didn't have human feelings: I hungered. I needed. I was greedy and grasping.

I crawled down Brad's body and settled against his thighs.

His cock was soft, curled against his thigh. I lapped at it to get it hard again. And it hardened so easily, growing into a towering length of flesh. I sucked him into my mouth. That was better, easier, focusing on the suction, the rhythm of my mouth, the action and nothing else. Just a means to an end. This was about fucking and feeding. Nothing more.

But then he reached for me. Tenderly. His fingertips ghosted against my cheek. "Open your eyes." His voice was soft, urgent with need and something else entirely.

I focused on him, sucking him and watching his face, his wide pupils. He felt something, too. And when he came, shooting into my mouth, his eyes finally closed under the pleasure of it all. I drank it all down, along with just a bit more of his essence. I was careful, oh so careful. I didn't take much. When his breathing grew even again and he watched me once more, we smiled at each other.

"Come here, Victoria." He hauled me up against his body and I pressed my nose into his neck. He smelled like the pinefresh cologne he'd splashed on earlier. Oddly enough, I found it intoxicating.

"Would you..." I started.

"Would I?"

"Call me Fanny."

He shook his head. "Isn't your name Victoria?"

"Fanny is my middle name," I lied. Tonight wasn't the time for truth. If he was fortunate, I'd tire of him in a week and he'd only lose a couple of years. If I grew more attached, we would play the confession game. But not just yet.

"Well, Victoria Fanny, that was amazing." He stared down at me, traced my lips with his thumb. "*You* are amazing. Tell me what you like for breakfast while we both can still think."

He wanted to make me breakfast? How sweet. Tears stung

my eyes, but I blinked them away. "Blueberry pancakes. Now, get some sleep."

We drifted off, languidly, in each other's arms. *I could get used to this,* I thought.

If he was unfortunate, I'd give him back the years I stole, plus all of eternity.

MOON LIKE A SICKLE, WIND LIKE A KNIFE

Jean Roberta

L et me in." Alison was at my front door. The porch light cast
a halo on her glossy black hair and drained the color from
her normally peach-toned face.

My heart lost its rhythm, and I clutched at my common sense.
I could feel my breasts jiggling under my nightshirt.

I recklessly opened the door, letting in a gust of cold air.
"It's late," I told her. *Insanely late for a social visit from a
colleague.*

"I'm not safe at home. The cops are watching me. Jane, I
need to stay here tonight."

No, I thought. *It's too dangerous, and I owe you nothing.*

The woman looked into my eyes, and I couldn't look away.
"I can't come in unless you invite me."

We studied each other for a heartbeat. "I want you," she
said. "You can't resist me."

Not knowing what else to do, I woke up.

Getting ready to face my students at the university, I was

sure I could smell Alison's shampoo, deodorant or moisturizer, mixed with earthier notes from her body. She had never entered my house, but she had invaded my mind. And parts south.

I parked the car in the lot and walked to the English Department. I passed Alison's office and felt stupidly disappointed to see the door closed, with darkness at the window. I enjoyed the cartoon image of Catherine and Heathcliff from *Wuthering Heights* taped to her door. Alison specialized in gothic fiction.

There were rumors. A month ago, she had come west to the local upstart university from the ivy-covered halls of an old Eastern campus. Her husband, a hard-drinking novelist who had escaped from an urban battle zone by means of talent and chutzpah, had tried to stab her when she confronted him about his groupies. There were headlines and a suspended sentence. Then he disappeared.

On my way to the classroom, I ducked into the lavatory to check my makeup and clothes in the mirror. "You look fine, Jane," laughed Alison from behind me. I lost any composure I might have had. "Good reflexes too."

I confronted my image. Everything about me looked undeveloped, from my innocent shoulder-length brown hair to my cow-like brown eyes to the modest curves under my conservative suit. I didn't think I looked young, just frozen in time.

Alison was voluptuous in a purple sweater and a scarf that framed her cleavage instead of hiding it. Her hips taunted and dared the onlooker to try stopping his or her momentum. Her lips were glistening ripe, but her eyes gave nothing away. Her hair was lush but severe in an asymmetrical bob.

I could imagine her in a flamboyant affair with a woman if she chose to take a break from macho drama. I just couldn't see her wanting me.

"Little Jane." Her mockery came straight from Victorian

Yorkshire by way of literature. Her arms circled my waist, and
I felt their steeliness through three layers of cloth. She squeezed.
I stopped breathing until the room spun, and I took a desperate
gulp of air.

"I'm coming to class with you," she told me. "Then we're
going home together."

So many responses came into my mind at once that I was
speechless. Finding no resistance in me, her capable hands
unbuttoned my suit jacket and groped my breasts through my
silk blouse. I flashed on an image of those hands around the
neck of a man, squeezing the life out of him, shutting him up.
Against my better judgment, I leaned back against her solidity.
I wanted her to carry my weight.

I had been married too. After a messy divorce, I had to pretend
I didn't mind seeing Dave, rock-musician-turned-conservative-
windbag, piloting his latest grad-student girlfriend through the
halls. I hadn't seen him since summer, but he was guaranteed to
cross my path, probably sooner than later. Murderous fantasies
were my consolation.

Alison pinched both my nipples, as if to wake me up. "You
like this." She was daring me to deny it.

If she thought of me as Little Jane, I would play the role of
a plucky governess confronting a presumptuous superior. "I'm
a lesbian," I told her. It was hardly a secret in our department.
"How about you?"

She laughed into my hair, sending vibrations down my back.
"I prefer not to label myself."

"I have to go to class. I'll be late." *No time for games*, I
thought. *I have a job to do.*

"Let's go, baby." She actually slapped my behind over my
decent skirt.

Walking through the halls beside me, she kept up a stream

of polite chatter. How were my classes this semester? Read any good books lately?

There was no way I could drive her off without creating a scene.

Explaining poetry to a roomful of first-year students with Alison's eyes on me felt amazingly perverse. "It's the oldest literary genre," I said over their heads for the umpteenth time. She smiled like a crocodile. "It's a performance art," I told them. "The rhythm and the sound of the words are often more important than the literal meaning. Feel the vibes."

At last I was finished, and the herd of students streamed past me, adjusting their backpacks with hands clutching cell phones. "Do you need to get anything from your office?" Alison sounded gracious, but in control. "We're going to your house."

"Excuse me? I didn't invite you." I already felt the invisible stroke of her interest on my clit. I hoped the dampness at my crotch wouldn't seep through my underwear.

"Not yet." *Oh, yes. I hadn't invited her in words.* "Do you really want me to leave you alone?" Her dark gaze burrowed into my soul.

I sighed. "No. Do you want to follow me?"

"Honey." That described the texture of her voice. "You're coming with me, in my car. I won't let you out of my sight."

When we left the building, the wind caught us off guard. My suit-jacket wasn't warm enough, and I hadn't brought anything heavier. I wasn't prepared for the surprises of the day, including the sudden knife-edge of cold air that swept across the Canadian prairies to announce the coming of fall.

Alison's little Asian car welcomed me with its warmth. I watched her hands on the wheel as she drove smoothly to my house. I wondered if she had been stalking me.

I unlocked my front door. What if I threatened to call the

cops if she didn't leave? But I wouldn't. "Come in." So easy to say and so hard to retract.

Alison followed me into the hallway, pushed me against the wall and pinned my hands above my head. She pressed her mouth to mine. "Mm," she hummed in approval.

Give me what you have, I thought. *Fill me with a will as unstoppable as the wind. I'm tired of thinking too much and figuring out what I should have done after it's too late.*

Her tongue stroked mine, and her full breasts pressed heat all through me. "Baby. You could have asked me. Were you afraid?"

"We work together."

Her smile was cold. "Nah. If that's your policy, why am I here now?" She cupped my chin. "Want me to stop?"

"No, Alison." Her nearness made my skin tingle.

She let go of my hands to unbutton my blouse. My bra was no obstacle to her, and I soon stood bare-breasted with half my clothes on the floor. My nipples puckered under her gaze. She pulled off her scarf, and I noticed its design of little crescent-moon shapes. She draped it over my banister as though staking a claim.

"So much has been said about me, Jane. I can't be anonymous anywhere. Do you think I killed my husband?"

I forced myself to look into her smoldering eyes. "I don't know. If you had, I wouldn't blame you."

"Ah." She used both hands to raise my skirt. "Panty hose. You don't make it easy, do you?"

I rolled them down over my hips, kicked off my shoes and pulled the nylon off each foot. "There," I told her. My cunt had been hungry for too long.

Alison bent down to suck each of my nipples in turn. I moaned as she left them wet, hard and incredibly stretched.

"You've thought about it, haven't you?"

I thought I knew what she meant. "What do you think?"

Her strong arms enveloped me and she lifted me off the floor. She carried me into the front room, where she sat me down on my leather sofa. My skirt protected my ass from contact with cowhide, but wearing a vestige of my teaching uniform made me feel more exposed than if I had been completely naked.

Alison stood over me, holding a hunting knife. I hadn't seen her pull it from wherever it normally hid. Ice water filled my veins.

"I'm not going to hurt you, baby. Unless you ask for it." Compassion softened her face. She pulled the thick blade out of its sheath, and I heard myself inhale.

"Do you think I killed him with this? Or a gun? My bare hands?"

"I don't know."

"How would you do it? Don't tell me you never thought about it."

I remembered Dave's purple face, his mouth open in a yell. Toxic words poured out like smoke and lava: *liar, slut, pervert, stupid bitch.*

"Knife." *There, I said it.*

"I thought so. Let's try this." She crouched between my legs and spread my thighs apart. To my great relief, she pushed the sheath back onto the blade. Then she guided the cool metal knife-handle between my lower lips and steadily down into my wet heat. My hips rose up to get more.

She lowered her mouth to my swollen clit and nibbled it. The lightest touch of her teeth on my flesh sent me into orbit. My cunt clenched her weapon, over and over, as fireworks erupted in my mind. I was embarrassed to hear myself squeal. I knew I would find a wet spot on the leather beneath me.

Aftershocks still ran through me when the doorbell rang. "That's Dave," said Alison. "I told him to join us."

"*What?*" I looked at the front door, where I could see a tall, swaying body beyond the glass.

Alison used both arms to raise her sweater over her head, fold it and lay it on my coffee table. Wearing the black satin-and-lace bra of some Hollywood bombshell of yesteryear, she strode to the front door and opened it.

Covering my chest with my arms in a classic gesture, I looked at the man I thought I knew. I barely recognized him.

Dave's face was pale beneath the weed-like beginnings of a dirt-brown beard and moustache. He wore a paint-stained T-shirt and a pair of jeans with holes in the knees. He had not dressed like this since his teens. Beyond Dave was a dark sky studded with stars and a crescent moon.

Alison abruptly unsheathed her knife and held it under Dave's chin. "Strip."

He scrambled to tear off his clothes as though they were on fire. When he had removed every stitch, he dropped to his knees and crawled through the hallway into the front room, his cock and balls swinging.

"Jane, your ex-husband has something to say to you."

I hope it's something new, I thought. I was curious.

Dave struggled to look me in the eyes from the level of a dog: a collie or a retriever. "I'm sorry I hurt you, Mistress Jane. I want to make amends." He had an aura of exhaustion. Looking closer, I was taken aback to see red marks on his back, ass and thighs. Alison had been training him.

Well. Good for her.

"Jane, how could our boy please you?" Alison was enjoying this.

I understood something without analyzing it: she was feeding on our energy, mine and Dave's. But it wasn't the same in each case. She enjoyed controlling her playmates, whoever they were, but with women she could give back. Men were her prey.

I could learn from her. "Dave, I need your tongue." Throughout our ten-year marriage, he had told me he could never ever put his mouth on a woman's pussy because the taste was just too disgusting. And according to him, oral sex in general was too queer to be healthy.

He hesitated. Alison knelt briskly behind him, spread the cheeks of his behind and prodded his anus with the tip of her knife. He jerked. This was going to be delicious.

"Sorry, ladies," he mumbled.

I sat in the middle of my sofa, not needing to make room for anyone else. I raised my skirt to my waist and spread my knees apart, offering him the sight and the smell of a treasure he had never appreciated enough. "I'm waiting, boy."

Dave crawled to me and held himself steady with a clammy hand on each of my thighs. When he stuck out his tongue and aimed it at the general region of my clit, I was reminded of the leafy heads in medieval churches: pre-Christian images of the Green Man, or the spirit of natural maleness before it acquired a ridiculous ego.

After licking my outer lips, he used his hands to expose my inner folds. He explored them carefully, using a pointed tongue to seek out especially sensitive spots, and a flat tongue to reach a broader area. He lavished attention on me, and when my surging hips showed him how successful he was, he buried his face in my wetness and sucked my whole clit into his mouth.

"Uh," I warned him. "Too hard." He didn't need to know why I was especially sensitive at that moment.

"Why don't you ride him, Jane?" Alison stood watching us both with interest, her manicured hands on her creamy, naked hips. Nudity didn't make her look vulnerable. On the contrary.

"On your back, boy." He was good at following her orders. When he stretched out on the carpet, his boner stood up from its nest of matted curls like a sentinel. I laughed.

To my amazement, Dave didn't seem flustered or angry. Blushing, he sat up, crawled to his jeans, rummaged purposefully through the pockets to find a package of condoms, ripped it open with his teeth and rolled one over his hard shaft. He slid one hand slowly up and down it, looking respectfully from one of us to the other. He was offering us a gift.

I didn't need it, but I was greedy. I wanted to make up for lost time and opportunities. I wanted to remember Dave like this, instead of the way he was before. *Handy fucking devices aren't imitation cocks*, I thought. *It's the other way around. The real thing can be used as a toy.*

Maybe I was trying to convince myself that what I was about to do could somehow be classified as lesbian sex. Or maybe I wasn't interested in categories at the moment. I squatted over Dave, held his cock and guided it into me. It felt better than I remembered, like an energy bar for my lower mouth.

I could hear him struggling for breath when Alison straddled his head and lowered her triangle of untrimmed black hair over his mouth. *She likes hair*, I thought. I decided to ask her about this when I was less distracted.

I bounced on Dave's cock with increasing momentum, working up a catchy rhythm. Alison was doing the same in front of me, and I watched the movements of her firm, round ass. The slurping of Dave's tongue in her wetness showed how diligent he was. "That's it," she encouraged him. "Right there."

The whole room smelled of female arousal.

Alison clenched Dave's whole face with her thighs, and let out a throaty whoop that almost drowned out the sound of his coughing. My release sneaked up on me: one moment I thought I couldn't come again so soon after the last time, then the tingles in my clit triggered an explosion in my center. Dave groaned. In a second, his cock went limp and slipped out of me.

Alison and I stood up and hugged each other over Dave's prostrate body. His eyes were closed, and he wasn't moving.

The wind howled around a corner of the house like the sound of a woman's voice. "Little Jane." Alison's lipstick was smeared, and she wiped it off her lips with one hand. "You're beginning to see what's possible. He's not the only one who called me here. You know that, don't you?"

Did I? I felt so energized that it wouldn't have surprised me to see sparks coming out of all my chakras. I knew I couldn't understand the events of the day with my mind alone. *Could Alison read my thoughts?*

"Of course. And vice versa. It works better when there's trust." She kissed me as lightly as a moth landing on my lips, but with a hint of teeth. "Even the moon and the wind have things to tell you, baby. Do you believe me now?"

"Oh, yes." A deep laugh was forming in my guts. "Lover," I added. I had come to believe in the power of teamwork.

PHONE HEX

Elizabeth Thorne

*H*ades *Conference Room 7*
We need a new way to find victims," Anixana complained, as she called the meeting of the Succubus Circle to order.

"No one is practicing the old arts anymore," Derilia agreed. "I haven't been summoned in months. It's horrible. I've been reduced to picking up men in *clubs* when I want to feed." She shuddered delicately at the thought, her perfectly painted red mouth forming a moue of disgust.

"I like clubs," Yelena bounced into the room, her straight blonde hair falling past the hem of the short, sequined dress that barely covered her pert, round ass.

"You would," Derilia responded, glaring at her little sister's outfit until the ends of Yelena's hair started to smoke.

"I get to drink, dance, and feed on whoever I want," Yelena said, shaking out her hair so that the flames crawling up the ends turned into red streaks. "Only a few weeks ago, I got gangbanged on a pool table. When was the last time you had men that interested in you?"

"It's undignified."

"It's fun"

"It's inefficient."

The two sisters quieted instantly at the interruption of a new voice to their circle, and they opened their mouths in astonishment as a figure they'd never seen before entered the hall.

The succubus who commanded their attention shone with power in a way that the other demons had forgotten was even possible. Wrapped in formfitting black leather that hugged every one of her ample curves, her bronze skin glowed with health. Her eyes held promises that would tempt a saint to sin. Her thick black hair was as dark as night and so lush that, looking into it, one could almost imagine it held the stars.

"And you are?" Anixana stepped forward to meet the newcomer.

"The person who has the perfect solution to your victim problem." The new succubus smiled and sensuously stroked her tongue over her deep red lips. "You can call me Ruby."

"What do you mean, inefficient?" Yelena asked. "I get drinks and sex at the same time! How could that possibly be inefficient?"

"When you feed outside a circle of summoning, the power exchange isn't as complete, or as satisfying. That's why it takes a gang-bang for you to feel fulfilled."

"Huh." Yelena looked thoughtful, but then she shrugged. "Still fun, though."

"Which?" Ruby quirked an eyebrow. "The alcohol or the gang bang?"

The two grinned at each other in shared amusement.

"Don't try to teach your elders to suck power," Derilia interrupted, stepping between the two younger succubi. "We've been doing it since you were nothing more than a spark in the Devil's eye."

Ruby gave Derilia an arch look. "And I can see that you're doing *so* well.

"The trouble is, *ladies*," Ruby pointedly looked at everyone other than Derilia as she drawled out the word, "that you're not taking advantage of modern technology. The men are still out there. They're still driven by the same lustful urges. They just don't have the time or patience to learn the rituals of summoning."

"Technology has a cure for laziness?" Anixana sounded unconvinced.

"Modern men want to get their sexual kicks delivered to their home without any work. The Internet is an instant pipeline to the lusts of millions of men, and I've exploited it a great deal." Ruby stroked her hands over her hips and released a fall of glittering power. "Specially enchanted webcams got me where I am today."

"Please," Derilia scoffed, "that's no substitute for feeding in person and harnessing the power of a True Summoning."

"I agree," Ruby nodded her head toward the slender, boyish redhead, "which is why I've come to your circle with a different plan. I've created a virtual sexual summoning ritual optimized for mobile platforms that any man can easily access through a simple touch-sensitive interface."

"A phone hex?" Yelena popped up, excitedly pulling a small electronic device out of thin air and waving it at Ruby, much to the confusion of the rest of the succubi in the room, who clearly had no idea what their visitor was talking about.

"You got it." Ruby's amber eyes locked on Yelena's blue eyes in satisfaction. "I've eliminated the education and financial barriers. Summoning a succubus used to require years of study and esoteric ritual supplies; supplies that were difficult for most people to find even in more magical ages. Now, as the humans say, there's an app for that."

"So why do you need us?" Anixana's voice was curious.

"I don't want to deploy the app if it's not going to work, and I can only be in one place at a time. If I'm going to make this happen, I need other succubi who would be willing to answer the calls or the program will crash every time someone tries to use it while I'm already engaged."

"How will it work?" a voice called out from the back of the room.

"Men will be able to install the *Xtasee* app on their phone, which will be advertised as a method of entering a hypnotic state that simulates the best sexual experience of their life. When they activate it, the app will put them into a light trance while it runs a preprogrammed phone hex to summon a succubus using a virtual version of the Karenzikov ritual that was first developed in the fourteenth century."

"I hate that ritual," Yelena pouted. "It always turns my hair green. Couldn't you have used the eighteenth-century update?"

"I tried, but there were issues with cross-platform compatibility."

Yelena sighed, "I suppose I can make green work for me. Hell, I can make *anything* work for me. I'm in."

"Me, too," Anixana nodded. "I feel like I've been starving for centuries."

"Oh fine. I'll try it." Derilia glared at Ruby, "but there will be hell to pay if you screw this up."

"Isn't there always?" Ruby grinned. "Let's begin."

New York, NY

Alan was browsing the available apps for his new smartphone when he came across the icon for *Xtasee*. There was something compelling about the drawing of a woman's shapely torso on the background of a glowing pentacle, and after reading the description, he decided to try it out.

When he activated the app, a pleasant swirling image moved across the screen of his phone for a few moments. Just as Alan was beginning to wonder what exactly he was supposed to be feeling other than relaxed, a beautiful slender woman with long green hair and a short black dress appeared next to his bed.

"I can't believe that worked!" they both said at the same time. Alan blushed and Yelena's face blossomed into a predatory grin as she stared into his eyes.

"Oh, I *like* what *you* want," she said, climbing onto the bed and straddling him so that her dress rode up around her waist and he could feel the heat of her body pressed against his quickly hardening member. "I'm going to have fun with this."

Alan let out a brief noise of protest as Yelena reached for his phone, but when she didn't disappear as she set it down on his nightstand, he stilled, waiting to see what would happen next.

Reaching behind her, Yelena pulled a pair of padded handcuffs out of thin air, and quickly bound Alan's wrists to the headboard. Kissing him briskly, she climbed onto her hands and knees and turned around to do the same to his ankles, baring her naked pussy to his view.

Alan moaned and strained happily against his bonds as he felt his cock grow even firmer at the sight.

"You have nice fantasies," Yelena said, as she straddled him once more and pulled her dress over her head. "Being used as a tool for a woman's pleasure; having her take you however she wants while you can do nothing to protest. I can get a lot of mileage out of that." She smiled and ground her wet heat against the hardness in Alan's pants.

Alan desperately pressed his hips up against the woman who was sitting astride him as she slowly unbuttoned his shirt.

"That feels good," she said, seeming to grow more attractive by the moment. "Your need is delicious."

Alan whimpered as she moved down his body to open his trousers and let his erection spring free.

"What a pretty cock you have," Yelena said, and licked her lips. "But I don't think you're ready for me to use it just yet, are you? I think you want this to last a little longer."

Alan nodded and he sighed in happiness as the vision of beauty he had summoned from his phone delicately spread her soft folds with her hands and lowered herself onto his face.

Yelena moaned as Alan put his mouth to work, gently caressing her inner lips with his tongue before sucking her clitoris deeply into his mouth. Every moment he spent worshipping her body increased her feeling of strength and well-being, and as she let him bring her to orgasm after orgasm, her skin began to glow with pleasure.

"Well done," she said, and Alan licked his lips in satisfaction, trying to keep the taste of her arousal on his tongue.

Yelena smiled as she looked down at him, "I think you're ready for me to fuck you. Aren't you Alan?"

"Yes, Mistress." He blushed as he spoke aloud the words that he'd only ever imagined saying in his dreams.

"Good boy," she said, and she lowered her body onto his cock.

Alan cried out as she sheathed him in her moist heat, working his body into hers in agonizing slowness as he strained upward, trying to push all the way inside her.

Yelena wouldn't let him take control. She held him down

with what seemed like incredible strength as she fucked Alan the way she wanted, the way he'd always dreamed about, grinding against him in the way that brought her the most pleasure until he felt her inner walls contract around his cock.

Suddenly Alan's bonds disappeared, and he flipped her onto her back, brought her legs to his shoulders, and fucked her deeply until he reached his own orgasm.

The moment he came she disappeared. Alan didn't return to consciousness for three days.

Los Angeles, CA
Anixana was surprised to find herself materializing in a small, but private, public bathroom with the logo of a famous coffee chain stenciled prominently on the mirror. Before her, a well-dressed and fully clothed, man leaned on the wall by the toilet, holding on to his phone.

"Holy crap," he said, "this really is lifelike."

Anixana blinked up at him, "You wanted to experience your sexual fantasy here?"

"I was curious." The dark-haired man gave her a rakish smile. "Besides, there's something I've always wanted to try."

Anixana gasped as the man roughly grabbed her by the hair and bent her over the sink so that her hips were in the air and her hands were pressed against the porcelain.

"Stay there," he said, and he flipped her skirt up onto her back, pulled her panties down to her knees and quickly pushed two fingers inside of her.

Anixana felt herself growing wet at the power of his fantasy and arced back against his hand as he fucked her deeply and roughly, reaching his other hand around to rub at her clitoris until she convulsed against him in climax.

When she felt him starting to put her clothes back in order

and step away, Anixana began to panic. Knowing that the spell wouldn't be complete until he had experienced his own orgasm and she had fed, she dropped to her knees on the filthy bathroom floor and started to unzip his pants.

"I never let my fantasies go this far before." The stranger smiled as she released his cock from its confinement and brought him to full arousal with a few quick strokes before taking his erection into her mouth. As she used her tongue to work the tip of his member, he took control again, fisting his hands in her hair and holding her head where he wanted it while he violently fucked her face.

Anixana could feel herself gagging on his cock as it shoved against the back of her throat, and as he came deep inside her, she swallowed the salty fluids of his satisfaction and realized that she hadn't felt so powerful in years.

When the coffee shop employees finally forced their way into the locked room, they found an unconscious man with his pants down and an enormous grin on his face. He came to in the Emergency Room, twelve hours later, with no idea what had happened.

Evanston, IL
James, Mark and Patrick were in their dorm room fooling around on Mark's new tablet computer when they came across the *Xtasee* icon.

"I want to see what that's like." Patrick said, reaching toward the glowing square.

"I don't know if I want to have 'the best sexual experience of my life' with two other dudes." Mark said, grabbing the tablet away.

"Could be pretty hot, though," James interrupted. "Triple teaming some hot babe."

"Or gangbanging her," Patrick said. "Two of us holding her down while the third has his way with her... Having some sweet little coed at our mercy all night..."

"I don't know..." Mark was hesitant.

"Come on, man." James slapped him on the back. "It's just hypnosis software, it probably doesn't even work, and if it did, we'd probably each be imagining our own fantasies anyway."

"We might as well find out." James opened the program before Mark had a chance to object.

A few seconds later, Ruby materialized, a vision in skintight black leather...until she quickly assessed the desires of the young men who sat gaping at her and changed into a short plaid skirt and low-cut sweater.

"You guys wanted to party?" she asked, summoning up the blush she knew they expected.

"Only if you do," Mark stuttered as the other guys glared at him.

"You bet I do," Ruby flashed him a warm grin, before turning to the other young men. "So how do you want to do this?"

"Why don't you start by doing a little dance for us, honey." Patrick smirked, and hit the button on the stereo behind him. "Show us those pretty tits."

Ruby blushed again and began to dance. Starting off with innocent shyness, she slowly unleashed the full sensuality of a succubus in her movements. She stripped off her sweater and skirt, leaving only a black-lace bra and matching thong.

As she spun gracefully around the room, she could sense the growing arousal of each of the three young men and could feel her desire building to match. *This is what it means to be a succubus*, she thought as she prepared herself to give in to their fantasies, *the need to give a man anything and everything he wants—and the ability to take everything in return.*

"I want you," she said to Mark, as the song ended, and she slowly lowered herself to her knees and gently reached out to open his pants and take his cock in her mouth.

Mark blushed in embarrassment, but Ruby could tell he enjoyed the feeling of her lips encircling his head and her tongue stroking along his shaft, even as the other guys continued to ogle them.

"Yeah," Patrick said. "Suck his cock."

"Arch those hips more," James said as Ruby worked her head up and down Mark's erection, making him moan. "Let us see how much you like it."

Ruby did as he asked, arching her back and reaching her fingers down to play with her own wetness, but she continued to focus her attention on Mark's pleasure until he spent in her mouth. Holding herself back from feeding too heavily on him, both because she liked the gentle young man and because she wanted to stay around to feast on the other two, she shielded him with her body, kissed him in thanks and quickly zipped up his pants.

"My turn!" James grabbed her head and forced it down on his cock, where it jutted long and slender from his pants.

"Hey! I wanted her next!" Patrick said. "I was going to fuck that juicy cunt of hers."

"Why wait?" James grinned at his friend. "I think she's woman enough to take both of us at once. Aren't you honey?" He pulled back out of Ruby's mouth just far enough so that she could nod in assent.

"Awesome. Patrick pulled Ruby's thong aside and shoved his thick cock deep into her with one thrust. "It's like we're making our own porno." Once he was well seated inside of her, he unhooked her bra and reached around to grab her breasts, before using them as handles so that he could fuck her the way he wanted.

Ruby felt herself glowing with the rush of power she was getting from the two young men, and she fed heavily on them as they each came inside her. *Well,* she thought to herself as she released her hold on the spell and let it return her back to hell, *I wouldn't want them trying that on some poor college girl.*

When Mark woke up the next morning, happy and well rested, he found his two roommates lying on the floor next to each other with their pants down and their cocks in their hands. The picture he took meant they would never try to push him into anything again.

Hades Conference Room 7

Raising her glass to the group of satisfied women who gathered around her discussing their adventures, Ruby said, "I think we can all agree that the phone hex is a rousing success."

Just then, Derilia appeared on top of the conference table wearing a furious expression, some smears of icing and not much else.

"Damn it, Ruby," she said. "I just materialized naked in the middle of a wedding! AGAIN!"

"At least this time you got to stay for the cake," Ruby said with a smirk, and she dove under the fireproof table as everyone began to laugh.

SOARING

Kate Dominic

The pretty blue scarf covering my hair and the lower part of my face served three purposes. It satisfied the local cultural mores. It kept the dust being kicked up by the front of our Humvee convoy from clogging my nose. And it provided me with a disguise that, for once, I didn't have to improvise on the spur of the moment. Other than being blown to hell by an IED, the only thing I had to concern myself with was protecting my camera and lenses as we jarred over the rock-strewn excuse for a road leading down into the valley.

The smell of silk and grit filled my nostrils in the blazing September heat. Insurgents were hiding in the fields by the canal. Their auras left a foul taste in my mouth. They were scared, viciously angry men, this particular group driven by opium as much as religious zealotry. Thus far, I'd avoided drinking from them. The few mixed in among them who were truly capable of emanating bliss were exhausted and underfed. I'd chosen millennia ago not to endanger joy, or lives, by drawing essence energy from those who did not have enough to share, at least not with me.

The soldiers with whom I was embedded, however—I smiled quietly beneath my gritty silk scarf. Their muscular young bodies were ripe for the picking, virile and well fed, their sex-swollen gonads begging for relief. For days now, I'd snapped picture after picture of them, my pussy creaming at the flares of yellow, orange, red—sometimes even icy blue or white—lighting the auras glowing like halos around them, catching reflections in the spectrums only my kind could see. Unlike many of my sisters, I did not have the gift of prophecy, for which I was profoundly grateful. I could not have borne knowing which of my dream lovers would not be shining with life and laughter tomorrow, much less drawn the essence from them to ease their way.

My gift was that of balance, the ability to drain the excess adrenaline from the balls, and thank the gods, the pussies, of warriors who, for whatever reason, did not regulate the hormones pulsing from their bodies. I fed off the aftermath of their battles, the hard-ons and wet dreams and nightmares, even their tears as they drifted into restless, jittery sleep. From them, I drank long and slowly, feeding their arousals, enticing their semen-swollen balls and juicing pussies to shuddering wet orgasms. In their dreams, I licked and sucked and fucked, leaching just enough pleasure from them to take the edge off the turbulent emotions raging uncontrollably through their psyches—enough to feed the empty well of desire inside me until I no longer hungered.

Tonight, I would be feeding well. After several days confined to base by the weather, my soldiers had been bored, their energies less sharp despite their fixation with sexual dreams.

The sun had barely risen when the first IED exploded on

the road ahead of us, injuring no one but getting the soldiers' adrenaline pumping. The early detonation angered the hidden men. Undamaged, we were too many for them to ambush. Four of them hid their weapons and met us, smiling, as we rounded the top of the hill. They carried no weapons, but no children or animals traveled with them either. Their sweat smelled of deceit, even to my human nose. I inhaled deeply, drawing in the scent of anger pouring hot and spicy off my sweat-drenched soldiers. The fear and battle rage had passed, leaving only heightened awareness and distrust, and blood pulsing through their cocks as the adrenaline drained from their systems.

The sergeant and lieutenant held everyone in check, keeping their men and the "villagers" talking until the emotions had flowed away enough for there to be conversation. In the cluster of houses beyond, the true villagers and eventually their hidden women finally came out, bringing children and rounded pregnant bellies and finally tea to the female medic who offered medicines and vaccinations. Ellis was three days from bleeding, hormones pulsing off her in waves as she looked into eyes and ears and took temperatures. I stood next to her, surreptitiously inhaling the perfume of her sweat as I took innocent pictures of the children for my publisher. After all, in return for my award-winning photojournalism, he paid my way.

When I was accepted enough for the elders to let me wander, I reset the settings on my camera. Still close to the soldiers who protected my body, I walked smiling around the village, tasting essences from those from whom it was safe to sip. From a doorway, I caught the pretty hazel eyes of a young woman, her belly swollen under a light blue burka that covered all but her face. She watched a handsome man perhaps five years her senior leading a young girl back to her. He had not been one of

those hiding in the field. He glowed with fierce determination
to protect his family.

The lust-filled gazes he shared with his wife had my pussy
creaming. He was wake-dreaming of spooning up behind her
in the dark, his cock sliding into her slick, wet pussy as his
balls rose against her ass. They were so hungry for each other,
for a fleeting moment, I let my vision blur, let my body go into
trance as I slid between their thoughts, licking between her
juicing folds, wiping the weeping head of his cock with my
tongue, feeding arousal from one to the other as my corporeal
pussy creamed and throbbed. But they were both too thin for
me to sup from them, not without exhausting them, and I was
too hungry to sample lightly.

With a gasp, I slammed back into my body, staggering just
enough to catch the attention of the soldier next to me. McCormick, my Humvee driver.

"You okay, ma'am?" His voice was thick with Alabama,
his sun-bleached red eyebrows gritty with sweat and dust as he
reached out to steady me. I smiled and pushed my scarf back
up around my neck.

"I'm fine, just a little thirsty." I drew my water bottle from
my pack, drinking deeply as he nodded approvingly. "The heat
here can be oppressive."

"Yes, ma'am, it can," he nodded. "Be sure you stay hydrated.
Sarge will have your ass if you get heat stroke. Beggin' your
pardon, ma'am. You know what I mean."

"I do indeed." I gave him my most winning smile, and then
went back to taking pictures until he finally turned away. The
sergeant was most certainly going to have my ass that night,
though even he didn't know it yet. He was devoted to his wife,
would never cheat on her. But he was lonely and frustrated and
horny, and he missed fucking her ass even more than he missed

burying himself in her pussy. They would share dreams tonight and both be better for it in the morning.

Behind me, McCormick was watching Ellis, again, his hard-on throbbing under his battle gear. In his mind, she stripped to the waist for him, her firm pink-tipped breasts glistening with sweat as she circled her nipples with her fingers. Then she was suddenly someone else, a dark-haired woman with big breasts and mocha skin from his hometown. He'd dreamed of fucking her since last summer, when he'd seen her in a bikini at their high school graduation picnic. Then she was a busty centerfold in the favorite files on his laptop.

Fuck, I love tits!

His thoughts were so loud, I had to hide my smile under my scarf. The adrenaline surrounding me was dissipating, but it wouldn't go away while we were on patrol. The levels rose again as we remounted and once more bumped deeper into the valley.

The late morning sun had the dog finding two more bombs. We waited, hormones rolling off everyone like sweat while the EOD team disarmed them. But I had no privacy to sup. The meeting with the elders of the next village went well, but we had barely arrived when I was pressed into service, my face carefully covered, to record the event. Then we were back on the road again. The others had eaten while we were stopped. Now my physical body was hungry, too. I tore into an MRE as we headed back to our outpost the long way, around a *safer* hill, despite the new storm approaching.

I was Hungry. McCormick was watching the road like a hawk, tamping down dreams of jerking off as the wind rose. His essence tantalized me. I wanted so much to drink from him. I couldn't distract him, but I could taste the reflection of his essence. I raised my camera.

A white nimbus filled my screen. My ears roared with a noise too loud to hear. I closed my eyes against a light too bright to see. Then I was rolling, tossed about against the side of the Humvee as my camera slammed into my chin and my chest. Then there was only dark.

I awoke floating in a sea of luscious sensation. My pussy throbbed, my body was alive with pain. Voices murmured around me. A man and a woman.

"Her veins are in the wrong damn place."

They're exactly where they should be. They just aren't where yours are.

In the stunned silence around me, I Reached out to them, Touching them, sipping strength from their shock as the door to the room opened. The sounds of a sandstorm raged above the radio operator's.

"Sorry, Sergeant. The helos are grounded. Nothing's flying until the weather clears." The door banged closed behind him.

"She can't wait!" The medic's voice rose, then fell again. Ellis was frantic, but determined to hide it. "McCormick can't wait either. We have to medevac them. Soon!"

Fear. Life-force fear. It was not a taste I liked, but I was so Hungry, I drew some in, for strength alone. Beside me, Ellis gasped. In my mind's eye, I saw her bowed back, her mouth open in horror as I Drew from her. Immediately, I released her, letting myself fall back into the darkness. I would not harm her.

"Damn."

They were all drawing back. Danger fear. My physical body was too weak to move, so I used my spirit, reaching, keeping my touch soft, searching for arousal. McCormick was on a bunk next to me, sedated, his morphine-laced dreams sparking bright on a sea of sexual fantasies. His essence was weak, though. Dangerously weak. In ways they did not yet suspect.

I *touched* him, for just a moment. Not *taking*. He was not strong enough for even a sip. So I let my thoughts wander to Ellis's pussy, to the hormones flooding from her system as her progesterone rose. I licked her clit, tasting the tang of her pussy juice. I sank my finger into her, wetting myself with her slick juices, my energy shaking as I lightly drew essence from her.

"Holy crap!" Her voice shook as she came on my hand.

"What the fuck?" The sergeant was too stunned to move.

And then they *saw*. McCormick's breathing was getting ragged, his life beat stuttering. I let my dream shape fly softly to him. I reached between his legs, slid my finger under his balls and between his nether cheeks. Ellis was beside him, panting, trying to control her arousal and her voice as she adjusted the flow of his IV.

"You're going to be okay, Mac. Hang in there."

I pressed her juices into him. He gasped, his breathing steadying. Ellis was close enough for me to *touch* them both now. I stroked into her pussy, drawing her essence onto my fingers, sliding it into McCormick. His body was too damaged for his cock to rise, but he was dreaming he was the man in a video he'd seen, bending over in front of a woman in a purple suede harness. The huge fake blue dildo in the harness glistened with lube. The woman was fingering his ass, relaxing him for her cock, stretching him and filling him with lube so he'd hunger for her.

Again and again, I played Ellis's pussy, taking her to the brink of orgasm, drawing her Essence forward.

"What the fuck is going on?" The sergeant was beside me, his hand on my throat. Danger poured from him. I was too weak to fight.

"D-don't." The medic's voice shook as she trembled beside

me. "McCormick's stabilizing. Whatever she's doing, it's keeping him breathing. K-keeping his heartbeat s-steady." She took a deep, unsteady breath. "It's just—whatever it is—it's making me come. A lot. Damn!" she shuddered as her pussy juice soaked her uniform.

Essence pooled in my palm. I slid my hand back to McCormick's anal gate. He wanted his ass filled, but he'd never done it before. His nerves did not know how to react.

The sergeant's did. He'd fucked his wife's ass for years. In a rush I saw he'd taken her harnessed toys up his own back door for almost as long. He knew the pleasure of a woman fingering his ass. I touched the pooled Essence in my palm with a fingertip from my other hand, slid that hand to stroke the curve of the sergeant's ass.

Spread your legs.

He obeyed without thinking. Then my finger was in. Deep. Curling up into his joyspot.

"Fuck!" he panted, his cock suddenly, gloriously hard. It jutted up, stiff and strong and full of life.

For McCormick's life, do not fight me. There is not time. Into his mind, I threw the image of his wife's beautiful blue cock sliding through his anal gate. *Share what your body knows, what it feels, that he might draw from your essence and heal.*

The sergeant gasped. Fleeting shock, then determination. His mind filled with memories of his wife's cock stretching his sphincters, drawing sensation through his anus as she fucked him long and deep and sweetly. He groaned, grabbing his crotch and squeezing, kneading the front of his sweat-soaked pants. His eyes were closed, his head thrown back. In his mind's eye, he was naked, standing on plush gray carpet, bent over a big, quilt-covered bed. His legs were spread wide, his hands braced on cool, soft cotton as he breathed deeply through his mouth, relaxing himself, opening his ass to his wife's cock.

"Easy, baby," he whispered. "It's been a while."

The sudden silence in the room was deafening. I drew breath into my burning lungs, my spirit hand moving back to McCormick. I hungered! It was so hard not to taste! Once more, I slid my hand beneath him, Ellis's essence glowing on my hand. The sergeant's Essence danced along my arms as I slid glowing pussy juice up McCormick's ass. He gasped, air and essence filling his lungs, power and energy surging into his body as it shared the sudden Knowledge sparking between us.

"He's stabilizing," Ellis said, her voice still shaking as she stood beside him, her hand on his heart.

And I was not. I trembled, releasing him lest I draw from him in desperation.

"Dammit." The medic's voice was soft, her hand cool on my neck. "I don't know what to do for her!"

Share. I thought to them. My voice was weak even in my mind. I was too far gone to hide myself from them anymore. My spirit shape flowed out of me, floating naked above my body, my skin swirling, fading as I reached for them. *Please.*

Suddenly, the sergeant was next to me, his hard-on pressing into my thigh as he rocked against me. Images of him fucking his wife seared into me, feeding me. Filling me. I sucked greedily, drawing his essence from him, unable to stop as his lust-filled thoughts flamed into me. His wife kneeling in front of him, sucking his cock down her throat as her long blonde hair brushed his thighs. Her lying in front of him, her legs spread as he feasted on her juicing pussy. Then her legs were around him, and he was fucking her. She was on her knees with her head down in the quilt, keening as she fingered her pussy and he plowed her gaping ass.

"She's a s-succubus," he gasped, bucking against me. "And she's too strong. She's dying. She's drawing too hard from me. She doesn't mean to. Think sex. Unh!" he jerked, his heart stuttering as his balls rose.

Share!

Ellis leaned over me, her breast against my mouth. I licked it with my spirit tongue, drawing the delicious power of feminine strength. She gasped and put her hand to her crotch, chafing the wet fabric over her still-sensitive clit.

More! I sent to her. *MORE!*

She gasped, images filling her mind of her boyfriend licking her, of his fingers pumping her pussy as she frantically rubbed her nipples. Memories of his cockhead leaking pearls of precum, of the salty tang of his thick, velvet steel cock sliding between her lips and caressing her tongue. Fantasies of him taking her from behind while a secret female crush from her volleyball team licked her clit.

"I'm gonna come again," she choked, her body taut, her breath coming quicker.

They were Giving too much. I could not deny them. And I *would* not harm them! I let my spirit fly, swirling through the outpost, stealing into dreams, seducing with hard, sharp spears of lust that resounded through sleeping bodies, through the guards on the perimeter, pressing orgasms from their healthy, virile young bodies, gulping essence—enough to tire, but not to kill—before lashing back into my human body.

It was still not enough. The body was too damaged. But now I was strong. I was bursting with power, more than enough to do what needed to be done.

Thank you. My essence glowing, I pressed a light kiss on Ellis's lips, on the sergeant's. Drawing lightly from them one last time, I let my spirit free. I touched my lips to McCormick's searing him with raw life power as my orgasm exploded into energy. Sparkling, shimmering power. His eyes opened, clear and aware, and I flew laughing into the night.

Below me, the body I'd worn went cold and still. It was no matter to me. I'd worn other shapes before. When I got hungry, I'd choose another. With a final puff of essence, I zapped the memory card of the camera and let myself soar with the stars.

ABOUT THE AUTHORS

NAN ANDREWS has been writing erotica for years, but she recently rediscovered her muse in Sin City. Her stories have been included in several Cleis anthologies, including *Where the Girls Are* and *After Midnight*, as well as Maxim Jakobowski's *Mammoth Book of the Kama Sutra*.

ELIZABETH BROOKS (EveryWorldNeedsLove.blogspot.com) taught herself to read at the age of three and started writing stories when she was five, though it took her a little longer to work up to erotica. She writes mostly sci-fi, fantasy and romance.

SASHA BUKOVA comes from a long line of poets, musicians and vagabonds. Sasha's mother escaped from Russia at nineteen, enchanted by America's love of free speech. A writer specializing in business, tourism and fiction, Sasha champions his family's love of free expression in the worlds of both fact and fantasy.

ANGELA CAPERTON (blog.angelacaperton.com) writes eclectic erotica that challenges genre conventions. Look for her stories published with Black Lace and eBury Publishing, Cleis, Circlet, Coming Together, eXtasy Books, Renaissance and in the indie magazine *Out of the Gutter.*

KATE DOMINIC (katedominic@gmail.com) is a former technical writer who now writes about much more interesting ways to put parts together. She is the author of over three hundred short stories and is currently working on a novel and several solo collections.

AURELIA T. EVANS is the author of several erotic short stories in such anthologies as Amber Dawn's *Fist of the Spider Woman* and Kristina Wright's *Fairy Tale Lust.* When she isn't writing, she attends school, makes jewelry, and watches horror movies.

KANNAN FENG (kannanfeng.wordpress.com/) lives next door to Lake Michigan and her current interests include Turkish cooking, circuses, and Heian Japan. She has previously been published by Cleis Press and Circlet Press, and is extremely fond of salmon roe, erotica, and the Oxford comma.

V. K. FOXE is a female/male writing duo who occasionally take enough time out from their kinky collaborations to get some writing done. They come up with twisted ideas together. Sometimes they cowrite, and sometimes one does the writing while the other cracks the whip.

MICHAEL M. JONES (michaelmjones.com/wordpress), editor of *Like A Cunning Plan* is a writer, editor and reviewer living in Southwest Virginia with too many books, a pride of cats and a tolerant wife. Find him in *Like A God's Kiss*, *Like A Queen* and *Rumpled Silk Sheets*, among others.

JAY LAWRENCE, an expatriate Scot living near Vancouver, is the author of twenty erotic novels and many short stories appearing on both sides of the Atlantic. Jay has experienced much of what she writes about and has lived to tell the tale! Truth, she's discovered, is often stranger than fiction....

EVAN MORA's tales of love, lust and other demons have appeared in more than twenty anthologies, including: *The Sweetest Kiss: Ravishing Vampire Erotica*, *Red Velvet and Absinthe: Paranormal Erotic Romance*, and *Lustfully Ever After: Fairy Tale Erotic Romance*. She lives in Toronto.

MINA MURRAY (minamurray.wordpress.com/) is a proud Antipodean and whisky devotee. She prefers Speyside to Islay, but is open to persuasion. She tries to find poetry in the everyday and can often be found with her head in a book (or in the clouds). Mina loves visitors, so please drop by.

CYNTHIA RAYNE is a multipublished author in many romance, erotic romance, and erotica subgenres. She currently lives in Northeastern Ohio.

Eroticist **GISELLE RENARDE** (wix.com/gisellerenarde/erotica) is a queer Canadian, avid volunteer, contributor to more than fifty short-story anthologies and author of dozens of electronic and print books, including *Anonymous, Ondine* and *My Mistress' Thighs*. Ms Renarde lives across from a park with two bilingual cats who sleep on her head.

Multipublished author **ANYA RICHARDS** (anyarichards. com) lives in Canada with her husband, kids and two cats that plot world domination, one food bowl at a time. The human companions leave her alone when she's writing. The cats see her preoccupation as a goad.

JEAN ROBERTA teaches English in a Canadian university and writes in several genres. Find her reviews at eroticarevealed.com and her blog posts at ohgetagrip.blogspot.com. She hopes her late ex-husband has found peace.

KAYSEE RENEE ROBICHAUD lives and writes in southern Texas. Find her in *Women on the Edge of Space*, *Women of the Bite* and *Cougars on the Prowl*. She has never successfully summoned anything but stomachaches and (occasional) story inspirations.

NJ STREITBERGER is the pseudonymn of London-based freelance critic and journalist Neil Norman. He began writing erotic fiction with a twist just over a year ago and was a regular contributor to the *Erotic Review*. He is currently the dance critic of the *Daily Express*.

ELIZABETH THORNE (WithBatedBeth.com) is thrilled to make her living from sex...writing about it, that is. In addition to her day job creating educational material about sexual health, she has published a wide variety of erotic fiction and nonfiction.

ROBIN TIERGARTEN (robintiergarten.blogspot.com) lives in Southern California, writes all kinds of erotica and loves to get dirty in the local Santa Ana Mountains. Recent Robin

Tiergarten stories include "Terra Cupidus" in *The Big Book of Bizarro* and "Recognition" in the anthology *Back Door Lover.*

Born in Amarillo, Texas, **J. S. WAYNE** currently resides in Las Vegas with his wife, Erin, and his puppy, Munchkin, where he is a full-time author of erotic romance, urban fantasy and horror. For more about J. S. Wayne's work, see his Goodreads page, goodreads.com/author/show/4766018.J_S_Wayne.

ABOUT
THE EDITOR

D. L. KING spends an inordinate amount of time reading and writing smut in her New York City apartment and postage stamp–sized garden. She is the editor of *The Harder She Comes: Butch/Femme Erotica*, *Carnal Machines: Steampunk Erotica*, *The Sweetest Kiss: Ravishing Vampire Erotica* and the Lambda Literary Award Finalist, *Where the Girls Are: Urban Lesbian Erotica*. D. L. King is the publisher and editor of the erotica review site, Erotica Revealed, which has been referred to as the *New York Times Book Review* of Erotica. The author of dozens of short stories, her work can be found in various editions of *Best Lesbian Erotica*, *Best Women's Erotica*, *The Mammoth Book of Best New Erotica*, as well as such titles as *One Night Only*; *Power Play*; *Lucious*; *Hurts So Good*; *Fast Girls*; *Gotta Have It*; *Please, Ma'am*; *Sweet Love* and *Frenzy*, among others. She is the author of two novels of female domination and male submission, *The Melinoe Project* and *The Art of Melinoe*. Find out more at dlkingerotica.blogspot.com and dlkingerotica.com.